THE BITTER HARVEST

For Colonel Charles Russell, former head of the Security Executive and now its *éminence grise*, watching the Middle East cauldron had always been another man's problem. Now it was coming to the boil, and many distinguished heads would lie easily for it, but not Russell's: to him it was still news, not business; interesting, but not professionally. Until the affair of Maurice Pater, and that was different.

Maurice Pater was a backbencher—would always be one, since he lacked the taste for the many little compromises with principle that open the doors to high office. A man of formidable, cramping integrity, whose views the House would hear with respect but never with fervour; a reasonable man; a man whose voice raised in a doubtful cause would do more to further it than the rantings of a dozen professional axe-grinders. So, if you were preparing for war and wanted a credible apologist in high places—and if your mind worked in a certain way—you went to Maurice Pater with a suitcase of used notes and let nature take its course. In theory.

In practice it failed, and miserably. They tried him with money, with blackmail, with violence. Maurice Pater was angry, sickened, afraid, but he hung on. He did more: in terms which astounded the House he denounced the cause he had been called on to support. To the plotters it seemed that they had delivered a dangerous weapon straight into the hands of the enemy; especially when Maurice Pater seemed in no hurry to return from a private visit to South Africa, a ready source of aid to that enemy. So Maurice Pater would have to die. Close behind him on his African journey came Georges Bresse, professional, fanatic, killer. And close behind Georges Bresse came Charles Russell.

The Bitter Harvest

WILLIAM HAGGARD

CASSELL · LONDON

CASSELL & COMPANY LTD
35 Red Lion Square, London WC1
Sydney, Auckland
Toronto, Johannesburg

First published 1971

I.S.B.N. 0 304 93792 4

Printed in Great Britain by
Cox & Wyman Ltd, London, Fakenham and Reading
F. 071

1

Maurice Pater disliked Saccone at sight. To Pater, a solid Member of Parliament, in the pinches potentially influential, Saccone was most things he loathed and distrusted—successful, materialist, smoothly commercial. Moreover his trade was Public Relations and rather a specialized brand of the product. Maurice Pater was meticulous and had checked his background carefully before he'd agreed to see the man. He'd very nearly declined to do so since on Pater's private scale of righteousness P.R. men wore horns and lashed their tails. They were dangerous—worse, they were antisocial—and the specialists fishing for Members of Parliament a great deal more antisocial than most.

But refusal had been out of the question. Saccone wasn't Pater's constituent but had a letter from a man who was, a very important man indeed, and Maurice Pater couldn't afford to offend him. Since Miriam, his wife, had left him he'd had little but his Member's stipend, eked out by some not very paying journalism. He couldn't afford to offend constituents, particularly Trade Union officials. He would have liked to, though; he hated P.R. men. He hadn't gone far as a politician, but one thing he'd always been, incorruptible, and if a mocking voice made the cynical comment, to Pater that voice was quite inaudible.

So Saccone came into the flat and sat down. 'It's kind of you to see me,' he said. The accent was Mediterranean but what Maurice Pater caught was the ominous 'kind', and privately and helplessly he bitterly resented it. Saccone didn't mean 'kind' at all. With that letter from that old fool Anders he'd know that Pater would have to receive him.

'If I can help you please tell me how.'

'Members,' Julius Saccone said, 'must be very busy men indeed. You'd prefer that I came to the point at once?'

'That usually saves time in the end.' Pater said it without a smile, as a fact. He had a sense of humour but not a sharp one.

But Saccone didn't come to the point: instead he asked an alarming question. 'May I know where you stand on the Middle East?'

Maurice Pater was cross but contrived to hide it for in the shadows old Anders's bland face was watching. 'What part of the Middle East do you mean?'

'I mean Israel and the Arab states.'

'Great wrongs have been done by each side to the other.' It sounded like the opening phrase of a particularly well-balanced speech. Well-balanced speeches had always come easily. They never set the House on fire, nods rather than cheers were their usual meed, but somebody had to preserve his judgement, somebody sane and somebody honest, some-one immune to pressure and interests. Pater was proud he was quite uncommitted.

'I know that's the line which you've always taken.' Saccone leaned forward, suddenly dangerous. *'And that's just what makes you valuable.'*

For a moment the words meant nothing at all, then Pater's face froze in a gelid stare. He had checked Saccone's history carefully and in the process learnt more than some simple facts. Saccone liked you to think he was properly Latin, a Sicilian and of noble family. Of course he never used the Baron, he was naturalized and in England now, where Baron was a dirty word. But his accent wasn't really Sicilian, and if he were Sicilian then presumably he was Catholic too. Strange, then, that when he crossed himself he did it from right to left, like a Greek. That was something to do with the men treed with Christ, the thief who'd died unrepentant on one side . . . north–south, west–east. More than one man had seen him do it, for in moments of extreme emotion the Baron, if indeed he were one, would cross

2

himself like a nervous priest. But why a Catholic under sudden stress should cross himself like a pious Greek . . .

Maurice Pater suppressed the thought as irrelevant. There was more about Julius Saccone suspect than the fact that he claimed descent from Sicily but crossed himself in the Orthodox Church. He had a certain reputation and it was hardly one of delicate scruple. Well, he was in an unscrupulous trade. Pater said coldly: 'I know your profession.'

'I confess I'd have felt insulted if you'd pretended that you didn't.' The manner had changed, it was man-to-man. They were men of the world discussing business.

They were not—this wouldn't do at all. Give this sort of man an inch and he'd take a mile. Pater must put his foot down sharply.

'I think you said you'd have felt insulted. I could claim that I've been insulted already.'

'That wasn't my intention, you know.' The words were smooth but without apology. 'May I ask what insult?'

'You used the word *valuable*.'

'But that's perfectly true.'

'I greatly resent the implication.'

'Rubbish,' Saccone said astonishingly. 'I suggest we stop fooling.' He was instantly much more than dangerous, he was a formidable man with a hand of high cards. 'Your daughter's marriage . . .'

The Member of Parliament gasped and rose. 'I think you had better leave,' he said.

'And I think you'd better hear me out. Putting it in the crudest way I'm younger than you are, you can't assault me.' He looked at Maurice Pater calmly. 'Since you force me onto this lowly level, well, it's one I was once familiar with. I hope that you understand me.'

'Outrageous!'

'No, simply life.' The expression was almost reflective now. 'Your daughter is marrying into a very rich family, and it's a characteristic of the upper class, in England and on the Continent too, that the richer they are the more they want. We expect a girl to bring a fair dowry.'

Maurice Pater let the pronoun pass for the statement was disturbingly true. He had personal reason to know it was true since a fortnight before he'd been asked to East Anglia, to Maldingham, the Beech-Lyon home, and it was Richard Beech-Lyon who was marrying Barbara. Pater hadn't enjoyed the visit at all. The Beech-Lyons had been in merchant banking before they'd bought land and settled as gentry, and the grandfather of the present Sir John had been Lord Mayor of London, a potent figure, in the days when that ancient expensive office had rated an automatic baronetcy. Today they were very grand indeed.

To do them justice, Maurice Pater reflected (he instinctively tried to do everyone justice), they hadn't patronized him or come upper crust; their manners were much too good for that, their techniques of communication perfect. But they'd beautifully made their position clear. Richard Beech-Lyon was a younger son so he wouldn't be inheriting, but he had an excellent job in the family business, a name and an established position. It was clear that the match was just acceptable but equally clear, though never stated, that for an elder son it might not have been. Still, if Barbara Pater married Richard then Barbara was marrying well, and marriage was a serious matter, a contract, an alliance, *business*. There'd been no talk of money, that wasn't the expert Beech-Lyon form, but simply, over the port one night, a mention of Sir John's solicitors. Of course Maurice Pater's would wish to meet them and of course they'd work out something appropriate.

The bland insolence had angered Pater, the cool though never expressed assumption that a man who spoke as the Beech-Lyons spoke, if not their peculiar County argot, would think as a matter of course of dowries, would indeed be able to lay one down. He'd been angered but he'd also been worried for he couldn't produce the ghost of a dowry. Even a rather grand wedding would stretch him.

It was tempting to think he'd been rather unlucky, but if your pride was an utter public honesty it was necessary to be honest in private, and it hadn't been wholly Miriam's fault that their marriage had broken up as it had. He'd been a barrister doing fairly well, politics really his second string, when Miriam had swept him away. He decided the phrase was by no means unfair. She'd been worldly and rich, a young woman of means, and politics had been in her blood. Like the Beech-Lyons though in a different way Miriam had thought of alliances first and a young M.P. would be clay to mould. He'd never supposed she wildly loved him but he hadn't supposed it would sour so soon. He suspected that in the end she'd pitied him, he wouldn't or couldn't bend or compromise. But if integrity was now thought old-fashioned to Pater it was his natural core. They had broken over that junior ministership, the first step on the ladder he knew she desired. Pater didn't admire the Minister and he couldn't serve with a man whom he didn't respect. The offer had never come again.

So she'd left him and married Lester Meyer. Johannesburg was a long way away, she never wrote and he never saw her. Perhaps she'd treated him badly, perhaps he'd failed her; he hadn't been blind and he'd known what she wanted, but in the crises he'd clung grimly to what he felt was his essential nature. That was the way he was made, God help him.

He shrugged but not quite with resignation.... Fault? That was something in the ultimate judgement for such gods as might be still surviving, but the facts had been left in the wake of the wreck and in the circumstances they weren't easy to live with. His daughter was marrying well, undeniably, and he was expected to find an appropriate *dot*. He hadn't the faintest hope of doing so. When his marriage had crashed he'd gone back to the Bar, but he'd been another political failure returning, a dog to a basket another had taken; he hadn't been wanted, he hadn't made it. Now he had his M.P.'s salary and a few hundreds a year from superior journalism. He could no more find Barbara Pater a dowry than he could buy himself a partnership in the Beech-Lyon bank he mistrusted on principle.

And this intolerable P.R. man knew it. He was bent on corruption and stating it shamelessly. He'd been silent while Maurice Pater thought but now he was repeating himself. 'The Beech-Lyons,' he was saying, 'will want a dowry.'

'I must ask you again to leave at once.'

It still sounded wet and Pater knew it. There'd be men who could deal with this wretched Sicilian, not sensitive men or men of integrity, but men who would know the right words and use them. Maurice Pater wasn't one of them, in a crisis he wasn't effective at all.

Saccone offered a cigarette and when Pater ignored it he lit his own. 'Better hear what I've got to say, you know.'

'I don't wish to listen.'

'I'm afraid you'll have to. It would be a reasonable question why I come to a man like you in the first place. You haven't asked it but I'll answer at once. It's because you're entirely uncommitted—uncommitted and widely known to be so. I was talking about Jews and Arabs. Both sides are already stuffed with supporters. There are plenty of Jews in Parliament, they don't have to pay for that powerful lobby, but the Arabs do and they waste their money. It isn't so very long ago that the Foreign Office was absurdly pro-Arab but the romantics have gone with the grosser pederasts, so if my clients want, call it, representation it's something they have to pay for in cash. And as I said, they've been wasting their money stupidly.' Saccone made a contemptuous face. 'Those Societies—they cut no ice. They're fronts and

6

are seen to be fronts by all. But you're a Member of known integrity and you've a platform in a journal of influence.'

Maurice Pater said coldly: 'You're trying to bribe me.'

'It isn't the word I'd have used myself but since you've chosen it I'll let it pass.' Saccone was offensively cheerful.

'You're trying to corrupt a Member of Parliament. That's an offence, you could go to jail——'

'Talk sense.' Saccone was being patient now. 'Where are your witnesses, where's the evidence? In any case you'd not face the scandal.'

'Outrageous,' Pater said again. It was one of his favourite words—he must watch it.

'Outrageous it may be but it's business. Now here is what we want you to do. There's a Foreign Affairs debate tomorrow and you can catch the Speaker's eye quite easily. You're respected on Foreign Affairs—that's why I'm here. You're respected because you're detached and fair but tomorrow you won't be detached and fair, none of that stuff about great wrongs by both sides. You'll come out hot and strong for us, after examining all the facts of course, prayer and fasting if you care to mention them. But you've seen the real truth at last and you've got to state it. No more sitting on the fence—your conscience won't let you. Reluctantly, but you've got to face it. Israel as a state won't do. You'll be listened to, indeed you will. And you'll run the same line in that paper of yours.'

'You're impertinent,' Maurice Pater said.

'I would be if I were asking a favour, but I'm asking no favour, I'm offering business. My clients may well be indifferent soldiers but some of them have a lot of oil and money doesn't mean much to them.' He looked at Maurice Pater squarely. 'Ten thousand,' he said. 'In notes, of course.'

Maurice Pater didn't answer him.

'I can make it fifteen.'

No answer again.

'Then twenty. That's final. It's not a bad dowry for any girl.'

'Go to hell,' Pater said. For Pater it was an extreme of abuse.

'Not just yet. I've a message.'

'Then pass it and go.'

'Very well, Listen carefully. There are more ways of killing a bird, you know . . .'

It was more menacing than a specific threat, the voice urbane but the face like a stone. Julius Saccone rose. 'Au revoir,' he said. 'We shall meet again. Myself or more likely the clients I spoke of.'

'I take leave to doubt you. Good afternoon.'

Saccone went back to his office and Bresse. Georges Bresse had been waiting patiently, the Arab in him defeating the Frenchman. He said in French:

'It went well?'

'It did not.'

'He refused?'

'He wouldn't even consider it. He would have liked to be rude but he doesn't know how.'

'You played it as we suggested—shock tactics?'

'There wasn't another way to play it. A man like that's something straight from the Ark.'

'No rest for the righteous,' Georges Bresse said reflectively.

'Then what are you going to do?"

Bresse told him.

'A bit of a risk, don't you think? Suppose——'

'Suppose what?'

'That's an offence under British law, a bad one. I want no further part in this.'

'You're not going to have one. Send us your bill.'

'I'm respectable now.'

Georges Bresse smiled wryly. 'Respectable so that it hurts,' he said.

.　　.　　.

It was late for a knock on the door but he went to it. Maurice Pater had views on the current crime wave and of course they were moderate, civilized, liberal. But this wasn't a well-policed part of London, and though criminals mightn't be wholly to blame it was senseless to invite a coshing. He cautiously opened the door on the chain.

A uniformed man was standing outside, peaked cap over eyes, erect and beribboned. 'Special Delivery, sir,' he said.

Pater looked at him and took the chain off. In the light of a street lamp the man saluted. 'Mr Maurice Pater, Member of Parliament?'

'I am. But it's late.'

'And this is important, they sent me by taxi.' He held out a parcel. 'It's quite a weight.'

Pater stared, uncertain. He wasn't expecting a parcel from anyone and this was a substantial one, solid and very carefully wrapped. It looked like books but he'd ordered none. He couldn't afford new books and seldom bought them. Certainly not in a pile like this.

'Who's it from?'

'Couldn't say, sir—they don't tell us that. They simply said to take a taxi.'

Pater hesitated but took the parcel. It was quite a weight as the man had said. He carried it to a table and turned. The man was still standing, holding a form out. 'Sign please, sir,' he said. 'Just the usual receipt.'

Pater signed and the man saluted again. 'Good night, sir,' he said, and went back to the taxi.

The wish was abortive, Maurice Pater's night sleepless. He opened the parcel but didn't believe it. Then he sat on the shabby sofa and shivered. Inside the parcel was crucifixion, the political death of Maurice Pater.

He'd signed for it too; he'd actually signed for it.

2

Charles Russell was dining with Harry Tuke. Russell had been head of the Security Executive and was now its acknowledged if unofficial grey eminence. Tuke was no longer Russell's Minister but the two men were very good friends indeed. Tuke was a politician, a pro, a man with a Party but not one he worshipped. He never hid his contempt for its intellectuals whom he blandly outwitted and sometimes crushed, but he needed a Party to stay in power and his loyalties were to power's necessities, not to theories or clichés like social justice. To the realist, and Tuke certainly was one, Russell was more than friend, he was natural ally.

Harry Tuke thought of Russell with real affection. Charles Russell had been an autocrat but also a wholly human one; he had the authority of a long experience but the humility still of the wish to learn, a man who had virtues he wasn't ashamed of but was prepared to laugh quietly at earnest abstractions. He wore a bowler hat in London since men of his age group mostly did, but Tuke had sometimes wondered what the conventional symbol really hid. A secret iconoclast? That was unlikely, but it wasn't a blindly conventional man. Russell knew the rules and he mostly kept them but he did so because that paid handsome dividends. On the rare occasions it didn't he'd bend them. A man from a very different world? Perfectly true and quite irrelevant.

They'd been dining in Russell's club in some state, and like most men who liked their food and drink they hadn't indulged in much talk at table. But now, in the smoking room, drinking brandy, Charles Russell said with an old friend's candour:

'I've seen you looking better, Harry.'

'That's what my wife says—it drives me silly. But coming from you I don't take it amiss.'

'The waterworks?' Russell asked with sympathy. His own

were regular as a Victorian clock but men who led sedentary lives could suffer. At sixty he was remarkably fit, with golf and a little fishing—fun. But not too active, he never pressed it. Absurd to pretend one was young still. He didn't.

'No thank you, I'm not costive yet. To tell you the truth it's simply worry.'

'But you've never been a worrier. If you had been you'd be dead by now.'

'That's true enough—I've mostly ridden it. But just at the moment it's riding me.'

'Then it must be pretty serious. Tell me if you'd like to, Harry.'

'It's the Middle East.'

'You're not Foreign Secretary.'

'No, but I think you know who is.'

Charles Russell replied by shrugging dismissively. The Foreign Secretary would not have been pleased for he rated himself extremely highly. 'But it's always been the Middle East.' Russell dispatched some brandy thoughtfully. 'Utterly hopeless but never quite serious.'

'You're perfectly right for most of the time but at the moment I'm rather afraid you're not. Would you like to hear?'

'Very much indeed.'

'Then let's start it as a matter of principle.' Harry Tuke, a good pragmatist, made a grimace. 'If British foreign policy can be said to have any principle it's the sensible one of not overreaching. It's taken some time to learn that lesson but by now we've got it nailed to the boards. We don't play in the big boys' league so we lean over backwards to keep out of their business. And in the Middle East Russia's probing hard.'

'You can't stop that short of major war.'

'In which we should disappear in a day, so we keep out on principle, just like I said. America might run the risk, of a first-class confrontation I mean, but only if national interest dictated. And America still has oil of her own.'

'But it's been like that for twenty years.'

'Quite so—real politics. Great Powers understand them and don't play them silly. Unhappily the pack has a joker.' Harry Tuke leant forward, his heavy face tired. 'Has it ever really struck you hard that there's more in the Middle East than Arabs? Also that in New York City there are almost more Jews than there are in Israel?'

'Certainly, and I'd call it unfortunate. Here's a vigorous, modern, extrovert people stuck down in the heart of a static Islam. From time to time attempts are made to throw them all into the sea but they fail. I don't know how many Arabs there are—some people tell me it's forty to one and others say that it's nearer eighty—but each time they try they bloody their noses. They're not a great martial race, you know, and intrigue is a rotten foundation for staff work.'

'Thus speaks the General Staff Officer—sensibly. It's what our advisers tell us too—a perpetual war which isn't one. But suppose they had backing, serious backing.'

'I suspect that you're contradicting yourself. You said that Great Powers don't play politics stupidly, which means that they try to avoid confrontations. Like Khruschev's gaffe over rockets in Cuba. And you trenchantly added another fact, that the Jewish lobby is very powerful. Do you think that fact isn't widely known? Throwing Israel into the Mediterranean would be something much more than a local skirmish.'

'I think you ignore one factor—hate.' Russell ordered more brandy and Harry Tuke drank some. 'The weakness of our sort of mind is that it strips off the leaves till it comes to the heart, then it sees that the heart is a stalemate and shrugs. But the leaves can be food to a hungry man and the Arabs are a hungry people. Hungry for what they consider justice, though you and I might choose rougher words.'

'What can they do, even with arms? They look romantic when they're all dressed up but they've a long way to go to make modern soldiers.'

Harry Tuke didn't challenge the wild understatement: instead he finished his brandy grimly. 'Egypt,' he said, 'means to close the Straits. They could do it too from Sharm el Shaikh. That would seal off the Gulf of Aqaba, and with the Canal already closed to them the Israelis would be locked in the Med.'

'You're sure of this?'

'As sure as I can be.'

'But the Americans——'

Uninhibitedly Tuke exploded. 'Don't talk to me of Americans, please! No sensible man is going to deny that if the Israelis were backs to the sea, on the beaches, fighting as we said we would but in fact were never made to try, then America would have to come in. She'd have to come in whatever the risk since there'd be more than enough internal pressure to force any President's hand wide open. But Aqaba, Aqaba, who's heard of Aqaba? Eilat wasn't even proper Palestine.' Tuke was cooling a little but not yet cool. 'An American President went to Berlin where he made a rousing speech about *ich bin Berliner*. It cheered the good people of West Berlin but it didn't impress a hard-boiled Frenchman. His name was de Gaulle and for once he was right. . . . So the Russians walk into Western Europe and we try to stop them with tactical nuclears. The answer to those won't be rockets on London, far less on New York or even Paris. But Southampton or Lyons would disappear. And if you were an American President would you risk Detroit for Southampton or Lyons? If not, would you risk it for Eilat? No.'

Charles Russell didn't elect to argue, they had had this discussion more than once. Instead he fell into silence, thinking, more interested in the military problems than in information

which might still be mistaken. But he didn't really think that it was for the story made dreadful political sense. ....
You were unwarlike and torn by internal rivalries and you'd several times failed in overt action, but you were forty to one and probably more and even rabbles would fight on their own harsh lands if you gave them the arms and the men to train them. So you went to a backer who'd find you both but you didn't again make the old mistake. You didn't attack your small neighbour—oh no; you took political action he couldn't tolerate, making it inevitable that he'd come at you if he wished to survive.

When the part of the world which didn't think would promptly shout 'aggression' and brand you. The part of the world which didn't think was unhappily rather a large one too.

Harry Tuke had been watching Russell think, relaxed again by now and smiling. He had a great respect for Russell's mind, even more for the way Charles Russell used it. It might indeed be a common weakness that both men looked first at the facts, not the words, but in a world which was drowning in abstract nouns Tuke found this congenial, even refreshing. He looked at his host with a real admiration. This distinguished and well-preserved ex-official had a horse sense which was much to Tuke's taste. Tuke was calm by now and he said quite normally:

'And then there's the domestic side.'

'Local politics that, and not for me.'

'No doubt, but it's something for me and I'm worried. I can guess what you've been thinking since I've been thinking the same. It's obvious. Israel's too small a country to fight on so if she doesn't accept to go under she'll have to strike. And that will upset the balance here.'

'I don't think I'm with you—not on the home side.'

'It's simple enough. There are more than a handful of Jews in politics and to me it isn't at all improper that they back their own people whenever they can. Equally the Arabs have spokesmen, and though they're very much third eleven they're heard. There's a sort of balance—we live by balancing.'

Russell was silent again: it made sense. Domestic politics weren't for him, in his official life that had always been true, but privately he followed them closely. Harry Tuke had a Party, not easy to discipline, and on an issue like this it could split down the middle. Not one of those publicized left-wing revolts which nobody paid attention to (nobody needed to pay attention with a majority as big as this one) but a genuine stirring of middle opinion, something which might indeed reach down to what was left of the Party's collective conscience.

'What could break up this balance you say you live by?'

'If somebody sounded the real silver trumpet.'

'That could happen in 1971?'

'It could and as Harry Tuke I welcome it. As a Minister of the Crown I deplore.'

'Some new Hampden to nail the flag to the mast?'

'Or some mute inglorious Milton in voice.' Tuke looked hard at Russell and Russell looked back. 'Have you ever heard of a man called Pater?'

'Yes,' Russell said, 'I've heard of him.'

He began to consider Maurice Pater. He'd had a file on him once, as he'd had on all Members, but it hadn't been the sort of file to give sleepless nights to the Security Executive. Maurice Pater had offered no danger whatever, he wasn't the stuff of spies or traitors. Russell remembered him not for the negative but for something he had respected—integrity. He wouldn't have used the word of himself but he'd had it and far beyond possible question or no government would have kept him in office for more than a couple of weeks at most. He could recognize and admire the virtue even when flawed by the man who owned it. The dossiers in the Executive had been a great deal fuller than files of fact and their picture of Maurice Pater, M.P., had been the picture of a prickly man. To begin with he'd been a lawyer and he'd had all the lawyer's private vices, the passionate love for what was written, the compulsive need to find a precedent. But though conscience, today, was a rare fine flower it needn't be paraded dourly, was much less effective if openly shown.

It was less effective? Yes indeed, but the fact remained that they'd listen to Pater, half in boredom at a material failure but also with a reluctant respect. Hard and wordly men would somehow listen, to the echo, perhaps, of what they'd lost or suppressed. Pater wasn't the Member to lead a revolt but he might crystallize opinion dangerously.

Charles Russell said: 'There are always the Whips.'

'I prefer you uncynical. Besides, it isn't quite like that. I've been in this business long enough to know that the Whip is a powerful weapon, but we don't put it on in a matter of conscience, genuine conscience I mean, the real thing.' Tuke flickered an eyelid and looked away. 'Returning your cynicism, we don't do it on principle.'

'Could Pater really fuse this bomb? He's been in the House for years and gone nowhere. No office, no following, no clique behind him.'

'He just happens to be an honest man.'

'In your world that's saying a requiem mass.'

'Nine-tenths of the time it's more than that.' Tuke wasn't offended, he knew his Russell.

'And the tenth time?'

'God knows.'

Maurice Pater sat down on the sofa and shivered. Inside the parcel was possible ruin, twenty thousand English pounds' worth of ruin in American hundred-dollar bills. He felt sick and faint, an inch from breaking, but he knew that if he broke for an instant the recovery would be near-impossible.

He rose at last and poured a drink. He drank little and for two different reasons: the first was that he couldn't afford to, the second a moral judgement of drinking. The drink, which was rare, therefore acted quickly; it gave him a small but effective dutch courage. There was indeed a debate in the House tomorrow and Pater still meant to speak in it. He knew exactly what he meant to say, he'd say what he'd intended anyway. Saccone could read it in next day's *Times*, and Saccone and his deplorable clients would know that they'd utterly, finally failed.

Saccone had been well informed, Pater caught the Speaker's eye quite easily. He wasn't a Member who made opinion but he stated it clearly if often dully—moderate, sound, middle-road opinion. Somewhere after the opening Minister and a couple of wild men on either side Maurice Pater rose and began his speech.

He began as he always began, rather quietly. The Middle East was a tinder-box and a spark could blow these countries to pieces, but this wasn't a matter for hopeless despair but for the action which they could take collectively. What was fatal would be a lack of decision, to allow this inflammable backward area to fall prey to a major Power's ambitions. For major Powers had natural rivals and those rivals specific and pressing interests. What was needed was international action. Yes, he knew there were observers already but much more was needed than merely observers. If the United Nations had meaning at all then it shouldn't be simply a fire brigade. It should act before the conflagration, and any member of a responsible government should back it with all the means he had.

He had spoken for perhaps three minutes when he realized he hadn't the ear of the House. He had never been able to set it alight but normally it would listen to him, with interest if something short of ecstasy, for if he was apt to be un-inspiring he was also sound and had studied his subject. But he'd been in the House for long enough to know that he had lost it now. On the front bench opposite two senior men were nodding openly and from his own benches behind him there was that ominous noise, a noise he had sometimes had part in himself, half rustle half murmur but wholly inhibiting, the sound of a bored and restless hive.

He frowned in irritation but was conscious he wasn't entirely blameless. He was saying what he had said before but it was still good sense, it needed saying, and if some of it they'd heard before they had always listened with decent respect. But it wasn't just what you said, it was how you said it; you had to put it across, the calm conviction, and his experience told him he wasn't convincing. He was talking of one thing, the Middle East, but thinking of quite another, his private life.

So they should act before the conflagration, and any member of a responsible government should back them with all the means he had.

. . . Miriam Pater—he hadn't been clever. She had taken him from the Bar too soon, she was a forceful and deter-mined woman. But he'd known that when he'd married her and a man should be able to steer a wife. There was a middle road between abject surrender and the hell of a frustrated marriage. Hundreds of men had found it. He hadn't.

Behind him he could hear movement now as they slipped from the chamber in twos and threes. On the front bench before him a man was snoring. A neighbour prodded: he woke with a start.

. . . And Barbara—that wasn't right either. Not this wretched affair of a formal dowry which the Beech-Lyons didn't need and would have to forgo, but the relationship between father and daughter. It wasn't openly bad but nor was it fruitful. They had lunched together the previous Tuesday for they had a standing weekly engagement to do so and she was scrupulous in keeping it. But that was all that he had of his only daughter. She never asked him to the flat she shared, she never dropped into his own without ringing. She had a job but he guessed that Miriam helped her, and certainly she saw her often, flying out for her Christmas and summer holidays, always at Miriam Meyer's expense. She never talked of her mother nor yet of herself. She'd never been hostile but nor was she loving. She treated him like a favoured uncle.

No, he wasn't very good with women.

On his own front bench a Minister turned, not precisely scowling but looking annoyed.

... And there was something about his daughter Barbara which he hadn't been able to place at all. She was marrying a man who loved her, you'd expect her to look happy, radiant. On Tuesday she hadn't looked even gay. He wished that he'd had a gift withheld, the power to read women's hearts as he read men's minds. Perhaps the pair of them had had a tiff. So they'd had a tiff but that would pass. Absurd to suppose that a sane young woman would throw away a splendid match because a busy young man had kept her waiting. And in any case it could hardly be that. Barbara Pater hadn't been simply piqued, it had been more than that, even he had known it. The word which had come to his mind was uncertainty.

No woman alive would ever have formed it. She'd have smelt out the truth at once, been excited. Barbara Pater had met another man.

Her father still had his peroration but the House was almost empty now and he cut it to the essential bone. Then he went home, aware of failure. Ten minutes later the House was normal.

He woke before dawn, the lights full on. Two men and a

woman were crowding his bedroom and apparently they'd come in by the window. One man had a briefcase, the other a camera. The woman was stripping naked fast.

The man with the case spoke in excellent English but with an accent which Pater couldn't quite place.

'So twenty grand was not enough.'

Maurice Pater said shakily: 'What are you doing here? And that woman . . .' He looked at her, then away in disgust.

'Don't play with me, please—you understand perfectly. You've taken our money and double-crossed us. From a man whom we'd bought that speech was useless. Just the usual soft clichés—not worth a penny.'

'You sent me that money? Then take it back.' Maurice Pater was conscious of sullen anger but also he was extremely frightened. The speaker wasn't the type of the usual bully but exuded what was much more scaring, the air of a total determination. Maurice Pater said, making time to think: 'Give a name and address and I'll send it back. The circumstances I'm prepared to forget. No prosecution, I promise you that.'

The lean face split in a sudden smile but it wasn't a smile Maurice Pater liked. 'You're a coward,' Bresse said, 'as well as a fool.' He turned to the man with the camera. 'Ready?'

The man with the camera had set up a stand and was loading a flash methodically. It was all very businesslike, very professional. 'I shall be by the time she's in bed.'

Bresse looked sideways at the girl and nodded, then moved to the bed and pulled down the blankets. The woman climbed in and posed outrageously. There was a sudden bright light and the click of the camera.

'No good at all.'

'Why not?'

'He's dressed still. Make him take off those revolting pyjamas.'

'Take them off, please. Co-operate.'

'I——'

Georges Bresse put both hands on Pater's collar. Pater thought he was going to choke him and flinched but instead he tore the jacket downwards in a single, a smooth and remorseless gesture. He seemed to have very strong hands indeed.

'Take off the trousers, please. Why spoil them?'

The Member of Parliament took off his trousers. The girl put her arms round him, started to kiss him. She had quite good teeth but the breath of the pit.

There was another flash and another click. 'That was better but it still won't do. You told him to co-operate.'

'What do you mean?'

'Just look at the man. If that's what he is.'

Bresse looked and laughed. 'I see the point, or rather I don't.' He spoke to the girl, for the first time uncertain. 'Perhaps if you offered some further encouragement . . .?'

But the woman shook her head at once. 'I think he's just a queer,' she said. 'Lots of them in Parliament are.'

The cameraman ventured helpful comment. 'Or perhaps if you beat him a bit it might do it. I've forgotten the medical name for it but I remember once I was doing some pornos——'

'I don't think that would work with this one.' Bresse nodded at the girl again. 'You'll have to get on top,' he said.

'I don't think you're a gentleman.'

'Maybe I'm not but I'll make it ten more.'

'But that way you'll only see my arse.'

'That's the idea—keep your face in the pillow. That way his own will be well in the picture.'

The girl climbed on top and the camera clicked again. 'Now that,' the cameraman said happily, 'now that I call extremely artistic.'

3

The type of man Georges Bresse liked least was a stout and over-prosperous Arab. This was founded on no romanticism, no belief, once sadly popular, that all Arabs should look like Bedouin sheikhs. He was half-Arab himself and knew better than that, but Said Abdul Jawal was offensively comfortable and moreover he was a diplomatist. Georges Bresse had very good reason to hate them.

He had been born in Blida of a happy mixed marriage, his father French and delighted to be so, and his mother, though Algerian, both Christianized and in outlook frenchified. They had lived the privileged life of their kind: the language of the house was French, their culture and thought entirely gallic. Georges Bresse had been at a French university when the doubts and then the disease had first gripped him, accelerating into a passionate torrent which had finally swept him to what he was now. In his youth he had been the typical Blackfoot and a little ashamed of his mother's blood, but as the merciless Algerian war dragged on, the reprisals and tortures and hopeless grim bravery, this blood had stirred, then boiled uncontrollably. Until he had finished his National Service he had spoken no more than kitchen Arabic. Now he was committed utterly, his career thrown aside without doubts or regrets, his frenchness no more than a useful cloak for his driving passion, the Arab cause.

So he looked at Said Abdul Jawal contemptuously, resenting that he'd been sent to London to work for a man he so much despised. Georges Bresse served a nameless organization. It was weak and divided, no match for the Israelis' Shin Beth, but money it could obtain—at a price. Money! What was money to blood? He despised these oil-rich easterners sourly. His own people had suffered and struggled and bled, fighting a military Power to a standstill, or rather a country which thought itself military. The people of the Mahgreb were men, these others were defeatist posers.

But one had to have money for serious work and this horrible man was one of its sources. He wore Arab dress because those were his orders but he didn't deceive Georges Bresse for an instant. He'd have been happier in a well-cut suit to match the glasses he constantly, nervously polished. This man was no more than a running dog of some anachronism who'd found oil on his patch and who now wasted what belonged to his race in a barbaric and utterly selfish luxury. To Georges Bresse with his disciplined dedication such a man was a traitor, no more, no less. . . . Not a village destroyed, not a moment of pain, just money he offered and never too much of it, money for Bresse's organization but a paymaster's insolent claims to control it. Georges Bresse loved the man who had somehow inspired it, but in London he had to take orders from *this* and he found it both frustrating practically and personally humiliating.

Said Abdul Jawal was saying smoothly: 'How did it go?'

'The corruption, you mean?'

'Let us start with that.'

'As I told you when you proposed the plan, you were misjudging the situation badly. More accurately you were misjudging the man.'

It was true, he had said so. The intention perhaps had been sound enough, for a man of Maurice Pater's standing could be much more convincing and therefore effective than any hot-gospelling obvious hireling. Which was exactly how they had tried to approach him. These Arabs, the Frenchman in Bresse thought. He winced. All men have their price? But it wasn't true.

'You instructed Saccone properly?' The voice was blandly arrogant and Georges Bresse would have liked to silence it finally. It wouldn't have been the first time he'd done it.

'Within the limits you allowed me, yes.'

'The matter of his daughter's marriage . . .'

'Was used since you expressly said so. I thought it another mistake myself.'

'May I ask why?'

Bresse sighed but hid it. He considered this man a clumsy fool who knew little of the English mind and nothing at all of a mind like Pater's. Pater certainly wasn't the stuff of heroes but he had an excellent brain, a passion for justice, and the Arab world had a very good case. So why not go to him and persuade him accordingly, show a lawyer the legalities and a notably upright man his duty? You might not succeed, you might half succeed, but that was better than this ridiculous bribery. Wave a bribe at the righteous—they simply went stubborn. This well-paid oil-sick man was stupid.

But not quite so stupid as to insist on Bresse answering him. He knew his past history and whom he now worked for and though, like all diplomatists, he formally deplored the irregular, he had heard of Bresse's record and secretly was scared of him. This wasn't a man you could safely offend. Besides, he had his orders which as it happened marched with his own inclination. Bresse must be kept in funds, he was useful, but the price of that help was both hands on the wheel.

So Abdul Jawal let the question pass. Instead he asked another. 'And then?'

'Then I did as you told me. I planted twenty thousand pounds on him.'

Bresse said it coldly, as a matter of fact, since again he'd had serious doubts and had put them. Planting money on Maurice Pater had in theory been an admissible ploy, but it had been the cleverness of the dilettante, the man who had read the books but seen no wounds.

The diplomat said triumphantly: 'And he took it. That is very good.'

'I don't think you can put it like that. What else could he do?'

'He could send it back.'

'To whom? To Saccone? Would Saccone have given him good discharge? I think that's the phrase the lawyers use.'

'But he signed for it,' the other said.

'He signed for a parcel, that's perfectly true.'

'Well, there you are.'

'No doubt, but where?'

Said Abdul Jawal was much offended; he paid Georges Bresse, he kept him in business, or he did for as long as he had him on loan. 'What more do you want to buy this man's help?'

'Not a penny. *Just fear*. So I used the alternative plan as well.'

'But without telling me.'

Georges Bresse didn't answer. He could see that Said Abdul Jawal was furious, but the emotions of a stout sleek clerk were unimportant to a committed agent.

'I shall have to report this.'

'By all means do so.'

Georges Bresse fell into a long calm silence, watching the diplomatist simmer. The alternative plan had been his own, and though he'd considered it far from certain he had also thought it much more promising than the one which this fool had insisted he try. Framing a man was better than bribery; framing a man could work—he had seen it—and there was also the nature of Maurice Pater. You couldn't bribe such a man with a million pounds but he was eminently vulnerable. The fear of loss of reputation, of the public fall from established grace. Photograph such a man in bed, his companion some squalid and obvious whore. . . . You had a chance if the precedents weren't all mistaken. But this absurd little man had turned that down. Georges Bresse cursed him long but wordlessly, reflecting that the clever boys were all the same in every country. They had a vast respect for what they thought was power, but power was much more than just *realpolitik*, it was how and when and a knife-edged judgement. Which this money-box didn't have and never would. Said Abdul Jawal had thought first of money, of the power of the purse and it hadn't succeeded. The man had been to Cambridge but he still thought in terms of trading camels. Georges Bresse who was half a Frenchman still had thought about a man called Pater, and when the first plan had failed as he knew it would he had used his own and had brought it off.

Or had he? One mustn't take it all for granted. He'd brought off the form of the plan without hitch but its result he would have to wait for with patience. Well, he had schooled himself in patience; he had learnt it in a French prison twice. He had never borne arms with his mother's clan nor lain out in the harsh and hazardous hills for his talents had been more valuable and his master had been delighted to use them. But twice he'd been caught and twice he'd suffered. When it was cold or damp he limped badly and he doubted that he'd ever have children. To the Muslim he now sincerely was this was the hardest to bear of all. But no, there was something harder than that, the patronage of this degenerate menial, the fact that he held the essential pursestrings.

Who had recovered some measure of plump equanimity. 'So you acted without even consultation. That is really very regrettable but if successful may be overlooked.' He tapped on the table, not looking at Bresse. 'Did you get photographs?'

'Yes, we did.'

'I trust they are good ones.'

'I think one was. Very.'

'Good,' the diplomatist said, 'so we'll use it.'

Georges Bresse had learnt patience a very hard way but

26

not hard enough to be quite impervious. 'We will not,' he said clearly.

'I said we will.'

'But I have the photograph. You have not.'

The diplomatist took his glasses off, polishing them while he thought it over. It was a gesture he'd learnt from a man in the Foreign Office but he hadn't yet realized the trick was ham. He might have broken Georges Bresse but he didn't dare to. Bresse had a long and a formidable record, and in the secret war they were both of them fighting, one from an over-padded chair, such men were too rare to waste or misuse, especially when the Israeli enemy could find twenty of them for each one you fielded. Georges Bresse was being impertinent to a man who by birth and trade was above him, but until he made a gross mistake, which all of them did in time, God help them, when of course you could take your revenge very easily—until he made his gross mistake he would have to be borne with and somehow suffered. That wasn't easy for an upper-crust Arab. Bresse's father had been a middle-class Frenchman and his mother had been, well, she'd been a Moor.

Said Abdul Jawal swallowed pride and spoke. 'Why won't we use the photograph, then?'

'Because if we have to we've certainly failed.'

'I don't follow that.'

'Then try to think. The object is to put pressure on Pater, to make him do something he otherwise wouldn't, to back us in Parliament, that newspaper too. So we threaten him with the power to disgrace him, to bring scandal upon his respected head. But we don't want to have to use that power openly. What profit to us is a discredited Pater? The uncertainty is our weapon, not action.'

'But suppose he does nothing, just calls the bluff?'

'Admittedly that's a possibility.'

'I prefer my own plan,' Abdul Jawal said.

'Which has obviously failed by now. This one has not, or it hasn't yet.'

'We could offer more money, raise the price. You never know with politicians and it isn't as though he were used to money.'

Bresse controlled his anger but only just. This man was a peasant and not a nice one, the sort who disgraced their common cause. The enemy sneered and was sometimes entitled to. Whoever has Arab for friend needs no enemy.

'You're wrong about the money. Believe me.'

'Since you're half a European I will.'

It was said as an insult but Bresse ignored it. From an equal he'd have exacted payment but from a creature like this he hardly cared. 'You've further orders?' he asked.

'You don't seem to accept them.'

'Then I suggest that we simply wait. Say three days.'

'And if Pater holds out?'

'We'll have to consider.'

'You'll keep me in touch meanwhile, of course?'

'I will since I must,' Georges Bresse said coolly.

Piet Brouwer got out of the bed and Barbara watched him. She lay with her hands behind her head, in the attitude, though she didn't know it, which the girl had first struck with Maurice Pater. She was exhausted, fulfilled and completely happy, the swirling undisciplined thoughts of a fortnight solidifying into an easy decision. Of course she wouldn't marry Dick Lyon. The idea was unthinkable, or, since she had certainly held it once, what it would be was asking for trouble, an inevitable, rather stupid disaster. Dick was charming of course, he had money and background, and unless you were an inverted snob it was foolish to despise these things. Barbara's friends had mostly envied but the closer ones had been somewhat surprised. Mary, for instance, had taken her hair down. . . . Was Barbara Pater really sure? She had an adequate job and a mother with money, an excellent figure, and she was twenty-four. In the terms of the friend who shared her flat that meant she was at the top of the market, but that market was something more than old hat and a wise girl wasn't obliged to play it. And Richard Beech-Lyon was, well, Richard Beech-Lyon. He too was at the top of his market so everything was just as it should be. Except that it wasn't—Mary was troubled. Richard was right, not a doubt of that, unshakably inescapably *right*. Right school, right job, right club—the lot. They came off the class production line as like as two frozen peas and as tasteless. Mary, a very old friend indeed, had finally asked the final question. Did Barbara Pater love this man?

She had said she did and said it firmly. Dick might not be a ball of flame but he was kind and tolerant, truthful and loyal, and what more did you want of a man than that?

Mary, who'd been married and mucked it, had snorted and gone on brushing her hair.

Barbara Pater rolled over lazily. She wouldn't think much of Richard Beech-Lyon whom she supposed she'd betrayed if that was the word for it; she wouldn't think much because she needn't. Richard Beech-Lyon was no problem at all, he'd do the right thing, he always did. Richard would release her regretfully, the perfect little gentleman, damn him.

Pieter Brouwer came over and stood by the bed. 'Are you hungry?' he asked.

'I could eat a horse.'

'That's a very good omen. Tea or coffee?'

She watched his wide shoulders across the room and in the kitchen heard him moving neatly. For a big man he moved with surprising delicacy. She looked at her watch: it was five o'clock. She hadn't woken at five for years and years, but then she hadn't had a man to wake her. In fact his beard had woken her and ten minutes later had tickled severely. She'd have giggled if she'd felt like giggling. He had one of those biblical all-round-the-chin beards, trimmed down close to the skin with his upper lip shaven, old-fashioned but superbly masculine, not the bushy badge of the boy intellectual but a badge just the same and he meant it so. It was the badge of a race he was wholly proud of. Pieter Brouwer was an Afrikaner.

('My name's Pieter Brouwer,' he'd told her at once, 'and you can't get any Dutcher than that.')

He came back from the kitchen holding a tray which he slipped on the bedside table carefully. There was scrambled eggs with mushrooms and a great deal of toast and butter, and coffee. He helped her and she began to eat ravenously.

'My God, it makes you hungry,' she said.

'And now you'll *have* to marry me.' He had asked her twice and she'd turned him down, once in Johannesburg staying with Miriam, and again in the last fortnight in London. He had known that she was engaged but been undeterred.

It hadn't stopped her either, she thought.

She didn't know how to answer him. From an Englishman this casual comment would probably have been made in irony but from Piet it almost certainly wasn't. She said at length:

'The Great Queen is dead.'

'So I learnt at school. Where I learnt something else about Queen Victoria.'

'Something about that absurd Boer war?'

'It wasn't absurd to us, but no matter. No, I learnt that my teachers weren't all-understanding. What puzzled them about Queen Victoria was that a just God allowed her to live so long. They were Calvinists, you see, as I was.'

'Was?'

'One gets older.'

The remark had been almost English in tone but she knew that a real experience backed it. He wore a beard which made her catch her breath and he was proud of his race and its dour independence. But he wasn't a stereotype—very far from it.

'So that's settled,' he said calmly. 'Good. I only hope that you'll settle too.'

'But I've been to South Africa.'

'Yes, I know. You've been to Johannesburg and you've been to the Cape. Johannesburg might be anywhere, some medium town in an American state, and the Cape is really another world. My people come from the low veldt— farmers.'

'But you work in Johannesburg.'

She had known this and that he worked for her step-father, for like the man himself his background hadn't been stereotyped. He'd come up to the Reef from the Orange Free State, a rustic with his two religions, Geneva and also rugby football, and in Johannesburg he had joined the police. South Africa had no formal riot squad, or not in the sense of the French or Italians, but the Brixton Boys had a comparable fame as the very rough lords of a very rough manor. He had told her that he'd soon tired of this and look-ing at him now, an adult, there'd been the flash of a private understanding. So he'd transferred to a branch which seldom wore uniform. About this he'd been notably unforthcoming and even more so about the circumstances which had led to his working for Lester Meyer. But he'd told her that he'd first met the great man at a race meeting where he'd been losing money. He hadn't much money to lose, had been scared, and he had known Lester Meyer by sight—who didn't? So he'd walked up to him bravely and asked for a tip. Meyer had looked him over coolly.

'I've a horse in the fifth. Don't back it at any price.'

'But it's the favourite.'

'Just so,' Meyer said. He'd made a gesture of polite dis-missal but Piet Brouwer had stood his ground and waited. Finally Lester Meyer smiled. 'It's a very curious country, this.' He gave Brouwer a hard but unhostile inspection. 'If I'm not deceived you should know that already.'

'I was born here, yes.'

'As you probably know I was born in London—Shoreditch, though you may not have heard of it.' There was a long detached silence while Meyer thought. Pieter Brouwer had the daunting impression that Meyer had simply forgotten him. He had not.

'In the fifth there's a horse called Wallenstein. The name should perhaps appeal to you.'

'Something to do with the wars of religion?'

'You're rather a curious sort of policeman.'

Pieter Brouwer was startled and didn't hide it. Lester Meyer was certainly Lester Meyer and would have information which other men didn't, but it would hardly include the identity of a young policeman who wasn't dressed as one.

'How did you know?'

'I didn't know, I simply guessed.' Lester Meyer's smile was now less impersonal; he seemed in some way to have made a decision. 'In London,' he said, 'I was once on the run. It was nothing very serious and nothing to what I've done here and been praised for, but it gives you a sixth sense for policemen.' He produced a card and held it out. 'If you should ever consider changing your job . . .' He smiled again and turned on his heel, then swung again as suddenly. 'Oh, by the way, that horse I mentioned. I run my own entirely straight, or rather I *think* I run them straight.' (That, he thought privately, does make a change.) 'But I don't train horses or sit on their backs and racing's no straighter here than elsewhere. So my own horse won't win, an angel told me, and if it does not I think Wallenstein will.'

'Thank you very much, sir.'

'Gladly. I look forward to our next meeting. Consider it.'

So Barbara had met Pieter Brouwer at Lester Meyer's magnificent home, her mother's too, who was now Mrs Meyer. He had clearly been a part of the household but it hadn't been easy to place him correctly. A strongarm? That was possible since a man with Lester Meyer's interests might have need of a strongarm in any country. But no, he hadn't the air of quite that, he was polite and he had read a lot, and though he'd told her he was an Afrikaner his English wasn't the stilted language of a man who thought in one tongue but spoke another. His clothes, she guessed, had been made in London, and he'd volunteered that he sometimes went there. For a holiday, he had said with a smile, but she hadn't entirely accepted that. Lester Meyer would have London interests, as he had in New York and in Paris too. They weren't the interests of making money which he did on a very grand scale in Johannesburg; they were the interests of giving money away. Lester Meyer was a dedicated and privately a passionate Zionist.

She had found herself sitting next to Pieter, and since she owned a tidy mind had mentally stuck a label on. This striking young man was the new Afrikaner, not liberal, that was a dirty word, but a man who had in a sense escaped. When he talked to his parents he'd talk with caution, for much that this man believed or didn't would seem treason on the dusty veldt. She would have liked to start talking of *apartheid*, but the rule of the house was a firm No Politics, and in any case she could guess the answer. *Apartheid*, this gorgeous male would say, was a philosophy before it was practical politics, and if you pressed him he'd rather the faithful defended it. Later perhaps when he'd known her better he'd have admitted that he had private doubts. The thing was an economic nonsense and in any case was full of anomalies. Moreover the latter made him look foolish and no Afrikaner would relish that.

So Barbara placed him as new Afrikaner, wondering

whether he read her as easily. He'd escaped and he was civilized, he was being very charming indeed, but at heart he was still what his blood had made him and she didn't have his people's virtues.

When he looked at her that didn't matter. She didn't have his people's virtues but she had something else and more important. It had taken him just ten days to propose. She hadn't been engaged at the time, but she had been when he had tried again. A persistent and indestructible people, like her mother's, Barbara Pater had thought.

Now he rose from the bed and removed the tray. When he came back he was very serious.

'We'll have to tell your father and we'll have to choose the right moment to do it. How do you think he's going to take it?'

'I don't know,' she said. It was scaringly true.

'I can't expect him to love my nation, but it's all in our favour he isn't stupid. He doesn't suppose that the streets of Johannesburg are crowded with white men assaulting Africans.'

'No, he certainly isn't one of those.'

'But he's a lawyer and that means he judges. He judges on the evidence as any good lawyer should and must.' He held her eyes with a total frankness. 'The evidence is mostly against us.'

'Some of it's twisted.'

'Some of it isn't.'

'You really feel that?'

'I must,' he said.

The telephone rang and he picked it up, his face setting suddenly, hard and decided. 'Very well,' he said, 'we'll come at once.' He returned to Barbara, still unsmiling. 'We're going to meet your father rather sooner than I expected to.'

34

'That was my father calling me? Here?' It couldn't be true, he couldn't know.

'He rang your flat, he was in a panic. Mary guessed where you were and finally told him.'

'Oh God,' she said. She was fighting panic.

'Your father,' he said deliberately, 'could be in very serious trouble indeed. Dress quickly please, and I'm coming too.'

4

It hadn't been easy for Maurice Pater to take his troubles to Harry Tuke. Tuke was in fact the Minister whom Pater had declined to serve with, not a senior one then but well on the ladder, and Pater had thought him not quite reliable, not really a man of solid principle. Now he was one of the handful who counted, and though Pater didn't know it yet not a man to bear a grudge or malice.

Barbara and Pieter Brouwer had found him an inch from a total collapse. Pieter had watched her comfort him, not explaining his presence nor offering comment, but listening to the broken story, occasionally asking the vital question. He had heard of this situation before, or at least of attempts to set it up, but would have confessed he had never met it in practice. So he'd have to consider the problem in theory and he hadn't a theoretical mind. But one thing was clear and he clung to it firmly: someone could now damage Pater severely but it wasn't yet certain they'd dare to do so. In the end Maurice Pater had looked at Barbara and Barbara had turned to Pieter. It hadn't seemed quite the perfect moment to explain that this was now her fiancé.

'This sort of frame-up can work,' Pieter said, 'but only if its victim lets it.'

'Then what am I going to do?'

'Sit tight. Sit tight and let them do the worrying. Let them worry what *you'll* do, not vice versa.'

'Not the police?'

'Not the police. The police would take details, they couldn't much help. They'd be just somebody else who knew the story. But if you've got some powerful connection. . . . Isn't there some friend in your Party?'

'I don't have many friends, just colleagues.'

'What about Tuke?' It was Barbara now. 'Didn't you once know him rather well?'

'I'm afraid we had a disagreement.'

'A serious one?' She was close to despair. So he owned no friends but only colleagues, he'd disagreed with a powerful Minister who could have made him if he'd been handled rightly. 'Would he refuse to see you?'

'No.'

'Then go to him when you're dressed. At once.'

They had spoken in unison, perfectly synchronized.

Pater had left Tuke quietly comforted. He knew that this senior and powerful Minister had resources which he hadn't mentioned, and though Pater had always much regretted that the world made their existence necessary, now it was pleasant to know they were there and that Tuke would know perfectly how to apply them.

He'd been comforted but not entirely, for there'd been something in Harry Tuke's calm manner which he hadn't been able to give a name to. The money had terrified Maurice Pater but Tuke had almost brushed it aside. . . . Potential political death? Oh, come. Really one mustn't exaggerate. Pater obviously didn't intend to touch it, so it was a matter of administration how he covered himself on the fact that he held it. The photograph was of course more serious, but on that Harry Tuke had been coolly practical. No reputable English editor would print such a thing this side of his grave, and to try for local publicity by slipping pullouts under constituency doors would be dangerous and might well misfire. But there was something else at least as threatening, devious but perhaps more effective, something from the Levantine mind. What had that man with the camera said? *I remember once I was doing some pornos* . . . Pornographic postcards—hm. Were there shops in Maurice Pater's constituency where you could buy such things if your tastes leant towards them? Pater hadn't known and had therefore said so and Tuke had looked at him in real surprise.

So there'd been something he couldn't quite pin down,

an instinct he wasn't a personal problem, just an awkward occurrence which Tuke must deal with. He must deal with it because of the Party.

And the reference to his constituency had struck him as decidedly ominous. Maurice Pater had a safe constituency, too safe, he had sometimes feared, for his good. The top men occasionally lost their seats or the Prime Minister wanted somebody in, and when that occurred Pater knew what followed. His safe seat would be wanted urgently and there'd be very effective pressure to get it. With good luck they would find him an outside job on some nationalized Board or some strange Commission, but they wouldn't do that if he made it difficult. If he did that then they'd throw him a peerage; he'd be Lord Pater of somewhere he'd once happened to live in. He didn't want that for he couldn't afford it. But now there were two strikes against him and politics was an unashamed jungle.

He began to think almost calmly now, assessing his enemies' possible action. It was how they would follow up that mattered. Tuke and that man who'd arrived with Barbara had both advised him to sit it out, but that wouldn't destroy that photograph, it could always be used in revenge or malice. He caught his breath, seeing these as the dangers—less action to exact an advantage than a rancorous retaliation against a man who'd successfully called a bluff.

Maurice Pater who seldom swore now did so. He wasn't very good at it but the words came out with authentic venom. It was the unfairness of it all which bit him. He'd done nothing to earn these strangers' malice, on the contrary he'd always spoken fairly. It didn't strike him as ironical that this fairness had been the bait which had drawn them: instead he simply thought them wicked. They had come to him and tried to buy him, they forced money on him as though he'd accepted. And that photograph . . . Maurice Pater shuddered. He hoped that Harry Tuke had been right, for Tuke had made no promises but a careful note of the shameful story. Then he'd smiled and confirmed Pieter Brouwer's advice. Maurice Pater must do nothing at all apart from keeping Tuke informed if and when (and of course it was still very much if and when) these people decided on further action. The ball was in that court, not their own.

That was true but it wasn't by any means final. These men were of different race, unforgiving. They hadn't forgiven the Romans, the Turks. It was centuries since the last Crusade but village storytellers still spun the yarn. Every empire in history had knocked them cruelly and they hadn't forgotten a single wrong.

He was conscious of an emotion which he loathed in himself and deplored in others. He was a very angry man indeed; he was frightened still though he hoped he had friends. Friends and a burning, increasing resentment.

Harry Tuke had summoned Charles Russell again and Russell had complied with mixed feelings. On the one hand he'd lost a round of golf which he'd been greatly looking forward to, but on the other it wasn't entirely unpleasant to realize that you were an *éminence grise*, that at sixty you could still be useful. Not actively—it would be foolish to try. He had never been what was called an operator and at his age had no intention of starting. Waving weapons had never been Russell's form, though occasionally, when he'd felt he should, he had gone with the men who had had to bear them. This was on principle, never for kicks, the principle of all well-run units that the commander who was never seen was a commander who soon lost his troops' respect. The Security Executive, whose delicate web Charles Russell had spun, had in any case regarded violence as a confession that other means had failed. It wasn't for the ex-head of it to set precedents which in his working life he'd have disapproved of and very probably disciplined. Just the same he had something more precious than weapons; he had thirty years' experience. So it was pleasant when men like Tuke asked advice, though the price might be a day's golf or fishing. Russell gave himself ten more years of life, of the sort of life he considered worth living. A day lost from this was more than nothing, but Tuke had stood staunchly by Russell in trouble and Charles Russell, if he could, would repay him. Not that his successor in office was anything less than notably competent, but Charles Russell had the name and experience, above all things the quietly effective connections.

To these substantives Harry Tuke would have added: his fourth would have been simply flair. The new man didn't have that just yet and maybe he would never acquire it.

For a man of small formal education Tuke told his story precisely and well. They'd been talking a few days ago of an explosion in the Middle East and had mentioned a Member called Maurice Pater. This Pater wasn't a Minister and he didn't lead a private clique, but he did have the sort of respect and standing which could be important if he decided to use it. They'd thought that together—*so had somebody else*. This somebody else had sent money to Pater to persuade him to beat the big drum for their side. Of course he hadn't done any such thing, so then they had tried to frame him brutally. Tuke knew all this because Pater had told him. He had come to him on his daughter's advice and on that of a South African whom the daughter apparently meant to marry. Very sound advice it had been at that, to come to the only Minister who'd be accessible to a man like Pater.

And controls the Executive, Russell thought.

But it couldn't be the Executive yet, not even on Harry Tuke's own orders. The Executive's charter was national security and that net could be cast very wide indeed, but take this story to Charles Russell's successor and he'd look like the civil servant he had been.... So a Member was being blackmailed? Deplorable. And how does that endanger security?

Russell sighed; he was going to be asked to help.

He walked to the Minister's splendid window, noticing that it wasn't quite clean. On the sill outside two pigeons were half-heartedly flirting, and as his shadow fell they clacked away.... Maurice Pater, a painfully upright man being bribed and then blackmailed to run a line. Lester Meyer who ran the opposite hard. His wife who had been Pater's too, their daughter and a man called Brouwer. Who was known to work for Lester Meyer though what he worked at was something less than explicit.

Russell didn't believe in increasing coincidence, and once he'd have been severely tempted. Now he simply wanted his golf and his fishing. Advice was one thing, hard slogging another, and in any case he thought Tuke had it wrong. He'd been worried about a split in his Party, was now worried about a possible scandal, but Charles Russell's thumbs were pricking differently. The danger wasn't the Party now, it could be one to Maurice Pater himself.

He turned as Tuke asked the formal question. 'Can you help us, Charles?'

'I'm afraid I can't.'

'But these hands do develop.'

'I know they do but I've earned my pension. I haven't so many years to enjoy it.'

... And the mayfly would be rising soon.

Russell put on his hat and went to lunch at his club. If he were asked for advice he'd give it happily but he wouldn't start wooing action at sixty.

As he went under Horse Guards a sentry saluted. Charles Russell took his hat off politely.... Harry Tuke had believed that this hand might develop. Of course it would, they always did, but he thought Tuke was watching the wrong horizon.

It was tempting but there was lamb for luncheon.

There was lamb and a comfortable chair in the library till the hall porter woke Charles Russell gently. 'I'm really very sorry, sir, but there's a very urgent message indeed.'

'From whom?'

'Mr Tuke.'

Charles Russell sighed but he went to the telephone. 'I'm afraid that I haven't changed my mind.'

'I didn't suppose you had for a moment but I thought I should tell you the latest development. We discussed something else beside our friend, the situation two thousand miles east of here.'

'And I ventured the banality that it's always hopeless and never serious.'

'I remember—for once I doubted you.' There was the pause of a worried and weary man. 'There's going to be a war within hours and there's nothing on earth we can do to stop it.'

5

When the Six Day War started Maurice Pater was shattered. He hated war on principle, sincerely believing what most men by now thought the crudest cliché, that peace in the world was one, indivisible. He hated war and he hated this one; he hated those who had clearly begun it.

Who weren't, except in theory, Israelis. You put a small State under wicked pressure, threatening one of its lines to the sea, then when it struck first you wrung your hands. Technically you might have a case but in practice it wouldn't stand up for an instant. Your case was sharp practice, your action an outrage, and you'd recklessly made it a great deal worse by the way you had put it forward. So-called experts had claimed special knowledge, but any expert who had happened to hear them had either crossed himself or reached for the whisky. Pater hadn't been worried by special pleading, any man had the right to state his case: what had worried him were the arrogant lies.

Normally he'd have examined his conscience since the organ was tender and he thought it important. But now he simply rang for a taxi. In it, for a second, he hesitated for a face had swum before him, his own. It was contorted in fear and a shocked disgust but it might also have been in naked lust. He hesitated for a second. No more.

Half an hour later he stood up from his seat. The House was crammed and decidedly restive for already they'd had a bellyful. Two mouthpieces had already spoken, each openly for his private interest, but the interest of each was known to all and neither had been in the least effective. The House was waiting for a Minister, waiting for news if despairing of policy, and meanwhile it was prepared to suffer.

Maurice Pater got up and looked around. A normal reception, he thought—no more. They weren't welcoming of Maurice Pater but again they were prepared to listen. He began to speak and in six sentences he knew it. For the first time in his life he held them.

Usually he began rather slowly, feeling his way to the first simple point, feeling the pulse of the House, its climate. But tonight Pater led with his right. It connected.

. . . A man must hate war. He'd said it. A cliché. What a man must hate was those who provoked it. Who in this case were not the State of Israel.

There was an instant reaction, to Pater astonishing. He had known that his Party was split on this issue, not the ordinary split of Right and Left, not even a straight split by race, but he had never sensed its depth and bitterness. Men he'd thought were his friends were grimacing angrily, and men he suspected of hating his guts were gesturing in open encouragement. For an instant Maurice Pater wavered, then the sense of the orator's power engulfed him, the knowledge he held them to do as he would. He'd never had it before in all his life.

. . . Great wrongs had been done by each side to the other. He'd said that too. It was true. And irrelevant. What existed today was a State called Israel and it lay in none of their mouths to deny it. A dreadful mistake? That was properly arguable. Also it wasn't the practical issue. For this House had been the Founding Fathers. It could not stand by while its child was murdered.

The answer was a noisy uproar and the Speaker intervened at once. It was quiet again and Pater waited. They were silent, expectant, an eager vacuum. Maurice Pater proceeded to fill it amply. He told them a little personal story, which was something he'd never done before since it wasn't his style and he'd never dared try it. But now the god had seized his tongue, he could say what he chose and these men would listen. So once, he said, he'd defended a man. He had seldom been in the criminal courts and this case had been almost a *cause célèbre*, so he'd only been a junior who hadn't

44

opened his mouth but had learnt the lesson. Two men had burst into a house one night and had roughly woken an elderly invalid. Who happened, understandably really, to sleep with a pistol under his pillow. The old man had drawn it and used it in fear. Not to mince words he'd shot them both dead, exposing himself in the process of doing so to a charge which in practice was plainly outrageous.

... As Israel was now vulnerable to a charge which was at least as monstrous.

There was another uproar, quietened at last. Maurice Pater was riding high and handsome. . . . There were law-yers in this House in dozens. He was one himself, he could say this properly. Beware the legal approach, forfend it. Israel had been a vast mistake? If you pressed him he wasn't quite sure that it hadn't, but that was water under a hundred bridges, this people had suffered, they'd taken little. Arab lands and the Arab refugees? One was nonsense, the other political pawns. The refugees had been a shameless scandal since there were States which could have absorbed them all without noticing that they'd even entered. And Arab lands? That was wicked rubbish. He wouldn't bore them with the history which admittedly could be argued both ways, but taking it as a practical question, what Arab lands and where? *How much of them?* Land belonged to the man who used it best. The goat had destroyed more empires than any army.

He sat down to something he'd never expected, a total and astonished silence.

But afterwards in the Smoking Room they came down on him like bees on a rosebed. He was praised, he was insulted, and he couldn't tell as a man approached him, he couldn't tell from previous knowledge, which line this man would ride nor why. There'd been Bentley, for instance—Pater didn't admire him. He had a sneaking respect for the real High Tory, but Sir Magnus Bentley was no High Tory;

he'd made a great deal of money and settled in the country, but no one quite knew how the money had come and no one quite trusted Sir Magnus Bentley. He was carrying two enormous whiskies and one of them he thrust at Pater. 'That was the stuff,' he said. 'Hot and strong. Time somebody said it, someone like you. Those bloody Arabs have had it coming.'

Pater declined the whisky politely, and when he'd finished his own Bentley drank it himself. 'Bloody Arabs,' he said again. 'Pack of rascals.'

Maurice Pater felt his bile rise strongly for he knew how the Bentley mind was working. In the war when Hitler was murdering Jewry Bentley would have been disapproving, or at least he'd have disapproved in public. Everyone else had been disapproving and Bentley wasn't a man with an itch for martyrdom. But Pater wasn't quite sure how he'd felt in private. Put him at a dinner table, with cronies, over decanters of port. . . . One doesn't approve of mass murder, old boy, but That Man does have a sort of case. Just look at his problem. I ask you. More port?

And now this problem people were a small but remarkable military power. Moreover they were bashing Gyppos and Bentley would relish that indecently. Of all the races his kind had enslaved none had been so despised as Gyppos, and when they'd grabbed the Canal they'd wiped his eye. With American assistance no doubt, against a military incompetence unequalled since the Crimean War, but the fact remained they had got what they wanted. Bentley hadn't forgiven and nor had others. So if someone was teaching these pigs a lesson that someone was Sir Magnus's friend. Never mind the rights and wrongs of it. Someone was killing the men Bentley hated, someone was doing his dirty work for him.

Pater sensed this thought and resented it hotly: the last man he wanted as ally was Bentley. Who was saying over his third or fourth double, not hiding a gloating offensive pleasure:

'The news is pretty good, what's more.'

'Is it?'

'Don't you listen to the radio?'

'Seldom.'

Maurice Pater would have liked to escape but he'd never been very good at discourtesy. He could see Magnus Bentley was determined to talk and he, Maurice Pater, would have to suffer.

'I heard it on the wireless.'

'Yes?'

If this horrible man would only leave him.

'If it's true then they've caught the Gyppos sitting—their air force on the ground, you know. I needn't tell you what that means, need I?'

He needn't, Pater thought—he'd seen it. It meant armour in a desert, uncovered, its supply lines destroyed at its enemies' leisure, whole squadrons surrendering, guns still loaded. Disgraceful? Well, of course it would be, but what else could the poor bastards do? A hopeless last stand? They weren't made like that. And as for the infantry, that would disintegrate. No infantry in the military world could stand unimpeded attack from the air, not Gurkhas, not the Brigade of Guards. They'd run and no man who had seen it could blame them, but their officers would steal their transport and that would be disgraceful as the soldiery had not been disgraced.

Magnus Bentley was happily droning on. 'So I'll tell you what will happen now.'

'If you must,' Pater said, but it didn't stop Bentley.

'They'll go through Sinai like butter but they'll stop at the Canal, I think. They could probably reach Cairo too but I don't believe they want to. I was in Cairo myself—in the war, you know—and no civilized human being wants Cairo.'

'You may well be right.' Maurice Pater hesitated. He was revolted by Sir Magnus Bentley but what he was saying was possible sense. Finally Pater asked: 'And then?'

'The other fronts? A pushover. They'll advance to the Jordan line of course, and then they'll take Jerusalem, though there may be a real fight for that. There's only one thing they won't go for directly. That's the Syrian Heights —they're quite impregnable. They're impregnable even with Syrians holding them. Not even Israelis will dare try that one.'

'I should hate it if it happened like that.'

'But I thought from your speech——'

Maurice Pater began to speak but stopped. It was pointless to try to explain to the Bentleys, their minds moved in a different world. To Pater it was bitterly simple. A crushing victory for this threatened State would be as bad in its way, though a different way, as the achievement of wildest Arab ambitions. He knew this people, he'd married one, this maddening, gifted, indestructible people who could do anything in the whole wide world except behave with an English moderation. . . . No negotiations but from a shattering strength. Put that against the Arab ethos which never forgot and never learnt, the Bourbons of the Middle East, and the great-grandchildren of men now dying would be dying in the sands in their turn.

Maurice Pater slipped Magnus Bentley at last and at home switched on the late night news. Neither side had made formal claims or admissions but the reports were increasingly circumstantial. A classic pre-emptive strike had succeeded, an air force had been destroyed on the ground. If this were true, and it seemed to be, then the war could hardly last a week.

Maurice Pater undressed and went to bed but he didn't sleep or even try to.

.   .   .

Said Abdul Jawal was saying angrily, 'The Western world is all against us.'

Georges Bresse couldn't bring himself to an answer. He was feeling rather French this morning and therefore sceptical of hyperbole. These moods sometimes took him but he wasn't ashamed of them, they didn't diminish his dedication. This stout clerk had it wrong. For one thing there was a Western Power which would see instant gain in denouncing Israel, in publicly breaking its formal contracts; and for another, if this man was half right, then the way the West was mostly reacting was the way Georges Bresse would expect it to. As usual his own side had talked too much; it had boasted and exaggerated. Talk of *jihads*, of holy wars, closed the Western mind in a frightened trauma since it had known its own wars of religion once; and talk of driving Jews to the sea was reckless and childish political madness. No doubt it would be watered down later. They hadn't really meant that —no, no, no massacre—it had been a figure of speech in the heat of the moment; what they really wanted was simply justice, a State where their people could live in equality alongside such others as cared to remain. Zionism was the enemy, not a faction which practised a different faith.

Georges Bresse hid a frown for the Frenchman was irritated. The Western world might well be decadent but it wasn't yet quite as besotted as that.

Said Abdul Jawal made another start. 'We shall have to do something about it.'

'What can we?'

Bresse knew what the man was referring to. Even Abdul Jawal would hardly believe that they could influence major events from an office; he was talking again about Maurice Pater. 'That speech was a disgrace,' he said.

'I confess it did surprise me after the line he'd always taken before.'

'I don't see why you're surprised at all. It simply shows I was right, you were wrong.'

'I don't follow that.'

'It's perfectly plain. To us he was valuable because he'd always been moderate, but that means he was also potentially valuable to the enemy who's now clearly outbid us.'

'You really think that?'

'Of course—it's obvious. I told you we should have offered him more instead of your ridiculous plan of bringing pressure through a threatened scandal, but you wouldn't listen, oh no, you knew better.' Said Abdul Jawal looked at Bresse with hate. 'The trouble with you idealists is that you don't understand how the real world works.'

. . . He's still thinking of trading camels, damn him.

Georges Bresse said: 'And so?' He was suddenly weary. It was pointless to break one's head on this stone.

'So we'll somehow have to shut his mouth. That speech of his was listened to and later it was widely reported. Then he did that wicked article, and though his paper hasn't a big circulation it has influence where it really matters. Pater is an enemy—dangerous.'

'So we offer him still more money now?' Bresse hadn't expected an irony would even be noticed by Abdul Jawal.

Nor was it. 'No.'

'Then what do you have in mind?'

'The time,' Said Abdul Jawal said portentously, 'the time has come for straightforward action.'

'What action?'

'I'll tell you.'

He started to do so and Georges Bresse listened; he listened till he had finished, then smiled. It was astonishing, he was privately thinking, that these men behind desks had this yen for violence. Georges Bresse himself had had to use it; he had used it and would do so again, but it had been a necessity not a stupid mystique, and if an ideal had lain behind it, then certainly he had paid for that. This rich diplomat had paid nothing at all, no prison, no men with those dreadful electrodes, no pain; he hadn't forgone a way of life, a half of the blood which ran in his veins; if he'd seen a corpse it had died of starvation and he wouldn't have creased his robes to check it. But he was talking of violence, of breaking Pater.

Georges Bresse said: 'Do you wish me to kill him?'

'I doubt if we need go as far as that. Just to put him into hospital and make sure that he stays there for several weeks.'

'You make it sound extremely easy.'

'I'm talking of what you're paid to do.'

Bresse wondered what the result would be if he quietly broke this dreadful man's neck. The beast was doing much more than anger him: the animal was an offence, he shamed them. He had talked about how the real world worked but knew nothing of what to Bresse was reality. Whose world wasn't cosy and far less secure. When his mother's strong blood had stirred in him yeastily, when the necessity had bitterly gripped him, dedication had seemed enough. It had not been. In the world of Georges Bresse one needed friends, above all things one needed an organization. His friends, to a Frenchman, were hardly reliable, his nominal organization a joke. It was split into factions by ancient rivalries, it was feeble and mostly amateurish, no sort of match for its principal enemy. One man kept him working loyally within it, one man and his unforgiving blood. But sometimes he wished he'd been born a Jew for then he'd have colleagues he really respected.

So here he was sitting, a loner, exposed—exposed to this insolent, money-sick diplomat. 'And you'll have to act fast,' this man was saying. 'The news of the war isn't good at all.'

Bresse had heard it too, as Bentley had, and his assessment wasn't so different from Bentley's. A defeat in the field he took almost for granted since he'd never thought military action hopeful. It was what would happen afterwards that Georges Bresse regarded with frozen horror. At the best they'd have lost several years of time and they couldn't afford several years of time. Israel would sit on its military pickings and Israel would bargain extremely hard. For the first time in her history she'd have strategic space and she'd sell it dearly. Very possibly she'd overplay it, in which case public opinion would swing, but public opinion, however it swung, stamped no armies from the stony ground. It would be an affair of guerrillas, armed men in strange uniforms, a bitter and savage and murderous struggle.

He had seen that once and Georges Bresse had loathed it.

'So you want me to damage Maurice Pater?'

'Within the limits that I gave you.'

'No.'

He looked at Said Abdul Jawal again, but not with the other's hate—with contempt. He was reading him with a cool shocked accuracy and what he read frightened him more than Israel. This man talked about necessity, of the need to shut Maurice Pater's mouth, but he was thinking in very much simpler terms, terrifying because they were also a weakness. They were a weakness to the whole cause Bresse served, this ancestral compulsion to take revenge. He had it himself but he policed it severely.

But then, of course, he was half a Frenchman.

Abdul Jawal was saying coldly: 'Did I hear you decline?'

'You heard me decline.'

'You cannot do so. Permit me to remind you, please . . .'

He went off on what Bresse already knew, putting it obliquely until Bresse cut in with the simple words.

'I know that you hold the pursestrings.'

'Good.'

'In your place I'd be proud to do so but I wouldn't assume I could buy stupidity.'

'You're impertinent.'

'Maybe. But I think your idea is extremely silly. Also I mistrust your motive.'

'How dare you insult me?'

Georges Bresse simply shrugged.

'You think because you've suffered a little——'

'No it isn't that, or it isn't the whole of it. We're just different kinds of men, that's all.' It was hopeless to try to explain: he left it.

'Nevertheless you're refusing an order.'

'You could put it like that.'

'I do.'

'As you please.'

Said Abdul Jawal said: 'I'll have to report it.' He had said that before but he hadn't done so. 'And what will you do without money, please?'

'Leave London as soon as I can, of course.'

'You believe that your friend in Paris——?'

'Yes.'

'I think you're going to be disappointed.'

'As my late paymaster you're entitled to think.'

The man at the desk tried another tack. 'And it isn't as though your refusal closed it. I can always obtain another man.'

'That, I'm afraid, I take leave to doubt.'

'I don't see why you should doubt it at all. After all I'm a diplomatist.'

'And you think that your diplomatic connections . . . ?' For the first time Georges Bresse laughed both loud and happily. 'Go to it, then. I wish you well.'

... By God it would be a classic shambles. He'd hire some broken-down thug from Christ knew where and naturally there'd be a balls-up. In any case Pater was probably guarded. If he'd told them that he'd been offered a bribe, if he'd told them about that photograph too. . . . That was useless now, like Maurice Pater, who wasn't worth further powder and shot. The sensible course was to write him off. He had made that speech and defined his position, and if he'd asked for protection he'd probably got it. This wouldn't have stopped Georges Bresse for an instant if he'd thought that this chairborne plan was wise. He didn't think it in any way wise; he thought it amateur and its motive suspect. Moreover he had the pride of his trade; he had killed without pity but was no man's gorilla. He didn't beat people up or torture.

The Arab flushed at the laughter but reined his rage. 'I am giving you a last chance,' he said.

'No thank you.'

'Then leave me.'

Outside in the street Bresse laughed again. His usefulness in London was finished, but in Paris there was the man he respected, the only man he wholeheartedly loved. He'd telephone and they'd call him back.

It didn't break like that, there were other plans. One of them was Said Abdul Jawal's. When Bresse had gone he thought long and wickedly. He'd been defied, called down, and the insult enraged him. By a man who was half a Frenchman too, and the other half was only Moor. Bresse would have to be dealt with and dealt with finally. You couldn't insult your betters and live.

Piet Brouwer, who was Meyer's man, had work which the latter had never defined. Lester Meyer owned several bright young men and Piet Brouwer knew well he was not the cleverest. What he was was an ex-policeman, trained, and

Meyer's enormous benefactions to a cause which not all men entirely supported could sometimes involve extreme discretion. Lester Meyer was a man of affairs and no sensible one made enemies foolishly. Hence Pieter Brouwer, the trips to London.

He was reading a letter from Meyer now.

DEAR PIETER [*it said*]

There is nothing which you could really call news, but there is something which perhaps is interesting. Have you ever heard of a man called Georges Bresse? He works for an organization which I am sure I need not name to you, and though I know you share my opinion of it, it does have just one or two good men. This Bresse is certainly one of them. Normally he is based on Paris, where the top man of his wretched lot works from. So I don't know why he is now in London.

I do not know and I shall not guess, but there are one or two things which might just be coincidence, and we neither of us trust coincidence. For instance, my wife's first husband has been behaving rather surprisingly. For a man who has always prided himself that he sticks to the middle way at any cost that speech he made was quite astonishing. Naturally we welcome it and it is not for me to question his motive. Whatever it was it was doubtless high-minded.

But if people like me are welcoming it there will be others who are hating his guts. I do not suggest a direct connection, just pass the thought for what it is worth. It might be worth half an eye on what happens.

Piet Brouwer thought it typical that Lester Meyer spoke of coincidence. Any other word was exaggeration. So Piet Brouwer would keep a discreet half-eye open. He'd have to, he thought, in any case, since he was marrying Maurice Pater's daughter. They had told Maurice this but they hadn't yet fixed it. Pater hadn't objected but nor had he blessed them; he had asked to see Pieter Brouwer alone. That was reasonable, there were reasonable questions, the sort which could hardly be asked before Barbara. So Brouwer was seeing Pater that evening.

At half-past six, he remembered. Good.

6

He took a bus to the bottom of Highgate Hill, then walked to Maurice Pater's flat. Piet Brouwer needed regular exercise and in London he hadn't had much time to take it. In the discreet and often urgent services which Piet rendered to Lester Meyer's cause time could sometimes be of great importance. A man could appear from Tel Aviv, from Amsterdam or perhaps from Naples, and provided he had the authority which Pieter had been taught to recognize, Pieter in turn had authority to give most if not all of what was asked. He also had the means to do so. Lester Meyer had quietly arranged all that.

He was thinking about his reception by Pater, not fearful since he had nothing to fear, but aware there was doubtful ground between them. He'd told Barbara her father wasn't stupid, not the sort who supposed that an Afrikaner went to bed with a *sjambok* and dreamt of its use, but there were policies which were plainly nonsensical and Maurice Pater wouldn't approve of them. They had a history as a private ethos, and if they comforted his parents' old age Pieter wasn't a son to smash the *lares*; if they made them feel happy, secure in the *laager*, then all you could do was to change the subject. Pieter was proud of his race, he bore its badge, but was no fonder of those awkward silences, the astonishment so politely suppressed, than were men who were far to the Left of him and whom he privately thought of as secret traitors.

All this, he'd decided, he'd put to Pater and if Pater didn't like it then Maurice Pater must do the other thing. Piet had nothing to hide but his work for Meyer, and if Pater had meant what he'd said in that speech he could hardly throw stones at another man's greenhouse.

Pieter found the house and climbed the steps, noticing that they'd started to crumble. This area had been prosperous once but now it was either decaying or arty. The well-to-do intellectual had been buying up the smaller houses, and they bore his stigmata like prints on the hand, the doors in defiant primary colours, the window-boxes in modern wrought iron. The bigger houses were split into flats.

Piet was looking at the name-cards when he was conscious of a man behind him. He hadn't heard him as he went up the steps, and as he turned with a smile he saw rubber shoes.

'Which number were you wanting yourself?'

'Be so kind as to ring the Number Four.'

Brouwer looked at the cards. Number Four—Maurice Pater.

He hesitated, an instinct alerted. Pater had said at half past six and it wasn't his habit to muddle appointments. This man could be a salesman perhaps, but he hadn't the air of the door-to-door drummer. Brouwer looked at him again with care. He certainly wasn't English but Pieter Brouwer couldn't go further than that. His skin was sallower than an Englishman's—a Greek perhaps, a Turk or a Cypriot. He wore a square-shouldered suit and those rubber shoes. Pieter asked pleasantly:

'You want Maurice Pater?'

The man didn't answer but nodded silently.

'But I've an appointment with Mr Pater myself.'

'So have I and it's an important one.'

There was nothing to do and Pieter turned. He pressed Number Four and waited quietly.

The voice came out of the speaker precisely. 'Maurice Pater here.'

'It's Pieter Brouwer.'

'Ah yes. Please come up.'

'There's another man waiting to see you too.'

'Another man? Who's that?'

Piet asked him. He simply shrugged and stayed there, waiting.

'He doesn't seem anxious to give his name.'

'Then he can't be of the least importance. Come up yourself. Shut the door behind you.'

The release latch clicked and Piet pushed the door. The square-shouldered man began to move. Behind him Piet caught the garlic breath.

He turned and the movement saved his life for the knife had already begun to move. . . . Hell, but there was a drill for this, he had learnt it as a tough young policeman. You blocked the swing with a forearm, chancing the wound, then you grabbed at the knife-hand and twisted strongly. He'd done it a hundred times in practice but the point was he wasn't in practice now. Besides, the knife had come up too far—you had to catch the hand early or not at all.

Instinctively Pieter Brouwer stepped backwards and inevitably he fell over the sill. He fell untidily, not at all as they'd taught him, and the dark face was above him, grinning.

The garlic smell was stronger than ever.

Harry Tuke had been in the House of Commons when Pater had made the speech of his life. He would have liked to leave after the first few minutes for he had realized the need of urgent action, but he was sitting on the front bench as usual and departure would have implied displeasure. He wasn't displeased or only mildly. Such a speech would harden his Party's divisions and he had told Charles Russell he didn't wish that, but with an open war now openly raging that hardening was by now inevitable. So if there had to be a split in any case it might be better to have it clearly defined. Maurice Pater was doing just that and forcefully. . . . This animal is a wicked one, when attacked it dares to defend itself. Such things needed saying and Pater was saying them, the more effectively since until this evening he'd done little but prate of peace and principles. That was how Harry Tuke had seen it.

It was characteristic of the Minister that he partly misread Maurice Pater's motives; he was certainly underestimating that behind this tirade lay an outraged conscience which as a driving force was at least as potent as the resentment which Harry Tuke took for granted. In any case he thought this clever. He had doubted that that photograph would in fact be used in any way, but if they did so then here was a valid answer. Maurice Pater was forging a useful weapon. . . . Scandalous photographs somehow get leaked so Pater in turn leaks the reason discreetly: it's a put-up job to discredit me since I've been telling the truth and that doesn't suit them. Credible? After this speech most certainly.

Harry Tuke had the emphasis sadly wrong for the mind of a man like Pater was alien, but a failure in analysis was irrelevant to the need for action. When Pater had finished Tuke left at once; he went to his office and picked up a telephone. An attempt to bribe a Member was one thing—for that he could hardly engage the Executive—and even when they'd tried to frame him it had been difficult to invoke Security. But people who could do either deed were people whose position was known, and when a dove turned suddenly hawk and struck there could be risks which Tuke preferred to eliminate. He would still have liked to use Charles Russell but he didn't think Russell would change his mind. So he picked up a phone whose line was secure and he rang to what Russell had once commanded.

He told the story succinctly and when he'd finished with rude photography waited. The comment was what he had always expected.

'Deplorable, of course. An outrage. But I don't quite see how the Security Executive . . .'

'Nor did I or I'd have rung you before. However, there's been a development.'

'Yes?' The voice was wary, an ex-civil servant's, but it wasn't in any way disobliging.

'Maurice Pater's just made a remarkable speech. It would be misleading to call it anti-Arab—he isn't the type to be anti anything. It was more damaging than that, much more. He simply told the truth as he saw it.'

'That the Jews have been there for as long as the Arabs?'

'No, he didn't bog down in disputable history. For Pater it was almost *realpolitik.* . . . Here's a very small strip of the Arabs' desert and another race has taken it over. No doubt there have been men displaced but their real hardship has been to be used as pawns. And to compound the offence of taking a desert this race has made it flourish notably. The money comes from you know where, from New York and Paris and London and Johannesburg. The offence is not the money, though, it's the fact that they're a modern people.'

'That's explosive stuff,' the polite voice said.

'A few years ago any Foreign Minister would have leapt to his feet and denied the lot. The present one didn't call Maurice Pater a liar.'

'He couldn't do that with very much truth.'

'In the Foreign Office ten years ago there'd be a posse of elders to insist that he did. Happily we've got rid of that lot.'

'And where,' the voice asked, 'do *we* come in?'

'You said it was explosive stuff.'

'Taking it from the beginning, the build-up. . . . No, I couldn't deny you have a point. Nevertheless . . .'

Harry Tuke said sharply: 'Nevertheless you'll be talking of policemen.'

'No, for once I shan't.' The voice was still bland but it carried an edge. 'I couldn't decently suggest the police.'

'I'm putting it as a request, of course.' Harry Tuke was a Minister, he knew Whitehall's language.

'Make me a proposition, Minister.'

'I'll make you a very modest one. I can't pretend I much like Maurice Pater but I'd be distressed if any mischief befell him.'

61

'You think it might?'

'Do you say it cannot?'

'Nothing so foolish.' A pause. 'Very well. We'll put a round-the-clock team on the watch at once.'

'I'm really very grateful indeed.'

'Not at all. A pleasure.'

Harry Tuke hung up and began to smile. The 'we', he had realized, was pure civil service, but the Executive was emphatically not.

The grimacing face was above him, arm raised, when suddenly the whole body collapsed. It fell across Pieter; he pushed it away. He got to his feet and looked hard at a third man. He wore a bowler hat and a very quiet tie and was picking up a rolled umbrella. The temperature was near the sixties and there wasn't a cloud in the blameless sky. He was using a curious pocket to stow something.

'The name's Edward Heath, though you won't believe it. Nothing to do with the other one, naturally.'

'Then thank you, Mr Edward Heath.'

'Forget it.' He took off the bowler hat and smiled, disclosing straw-coloured hair cut unfashionably short. 'I saw you ring Maurice Pater's bell.'

Pieter Brouwer could normally hide surprise but now he was shaken and didn't try. 'How did you know it was Pater's bell?'

'Because, my friend, I've been taught to make recce.' He looked at Pieter Brouwer coolly. 'I don't think we've met,' he said at length.

'I'm Pieter Brouwer.'

'Are you indeed? The man who's marrying Pater's daughter? They told me something of that but not a lot.' Mr Edward Heath considered carefully. 'In that case I think I'll tell you most things. I can't tell you who I actually work for, though if you guess it wrong I'll be much surprised. So this lot of mine puts me on to watch Pater. I don't know quite why, they don't always tell you, but obviously they were pretty damned right. I do eight hours on and sixteen off, which means another two bodies to make up the day. That's expensive in manpower, they don't like doing it, but in this case it was certainly worth it.'

'I didn't see you watching the flat.'

'I should hope not indeed—I'd be shamed if you had.' Heath added as a throwaway line: 'We all like to think we're pros, you know.'

'I'll give you that one.'

'You're very kind. So I noticed you and you looked all right and I noticed this bloke on the floor and he didn't. I'd guess he was Greek but we'd better make sure. Shut the outside door while I take a look.'

Heath bent down and rolled the other face upwards. The knife had been underneath and he took it. 'Dirty great thing— he's better without it. By the way, you rang up to Pater, didn't you? Perhaps he'll be getting curious, so if he starts to come down you nip up quickly. The last thing we want him to know is what's happened. If they think they're in danger themselves it's more difficult.'

'Understood,' Pieter Brouwer said, 'I agree.' An ex-policeman had taken the point at once.

Heath turned out the other's pockets expertly. 'No passport but you wouldn't expect it. But there is this letter.' He held it out. 'Now that,' he said mildly, 'was rather silly, to go on a job with a letter like that. Envelope too—that's really stupid.' He took out the letter. 'Can you read Greek?'

'Indeed I can't.'

'I can, or rather I read the characters, but I don't know a word of demotic Greek.' He looked at the envelope. 'Postmarked in Cyprus. That explains quite a lot in a rum sort of way.'

'Not to me.'

'You don't work here. These poor bastards come over in droves as waiters and England's a terrible disappointment. So some of them quietly drift into crime. Mostly they go for peddling drugs but a few of them take to the rough stuff too. They're a nuisance but you can't always blame them.'

'I can see that you're English,' Piet Brouwer said.

'I am indeed and in more ways than one. So I'm not going to guess who hired this bloke, that's another man's job and I'm not paid to do it. Strict Union rules, as you probably know.'

Piet had been watching the man on the floor. 'I thought I saw him move,' he said.

'I *know* he moved.' Edward Heath was impassive. 'He opened his eyes and shut them again. He's conscious but he's playing possum.'

'What are you going to do with him?'

'Get rid of the bod before somebody comes. Just open the door again, if you will.' Heath bent and took the other man's hand. 'Get up,' he said. 'Hup boy. Good dog.'

The Cypriot got to his knees, then his feet. Heath still had his hand but he also had Heath's. Piet Brouwer was watching his eyes intently. 'Be careful,' he said, 'he's not finished yet.'

But he needn't have worried for Edward Heath. The Cypriot's grip on his hand tightened suddenly. He tried for the arm-whip but Heath rolled neatly. He still had the other man's arm and pulled strongly, unorthodox and quite unexpected. The Cypriot bent since he had to bend and from the ground Edward Heath put both feet in his stomach. His knees had been bent and he straightened them powerfully. The Cypriot simply disappeared. He went through the door Pieter Brouwer had opened. He went in the air, limbs flailing, quite helpless. There was a sickening sound on the steps, then silence.

'Smooth,' Pieter said.

'But it's rather corny.' Heath picked up his hat and looked inside it. 'I hope he can move still,' he said. 'Let's see.'

They went to the doorway—the man was moving; he was raising himself by the railing, grimacing, using a single arm to do it. 'Shoulder gone,' Heath said. 'That often happens. Lucky he can use his legs.'

'He's lucky all right.'

'I meant for us. Awkward if he'd been left on our hands.'

Pieter Brouwer was astonished again. 'But aren't you going to book him?'

'No.'

'Look, the man had a knife and he tried it on me. He'd have certainly carved up Maurice Pater.'

'Which my job was to prevent. I did so. If somebody higher up thinks he's worth it we can almost certainly pick him up. If the name and address on that letter are phony then I've something else which will help a lot. Inside this foolish hat of mine is a peculiar but rather efficient camera. I don't think I bust it rolling, either.'

'It's not the only thing efficient.'

'Thank you. But I'm really not a policeman, you see.'

'I was a policeman once.'

'You were? I didn't know that. No offence, I hope.'

'None at all. I'm just learning, I quite see that.'

'Then you understand about Maurice Pater—not telling him about this, I mean.'

'But I may have to tell the man I work for.'

'Very proper too, it's always safer.' Heath looked at his watch. 'I've an hour and a half to go, then relief. Will your business with Pater take longer than that?'

'If I'm lucky again it ought to take less.'

'I don't think much more will happen tonight and after half-past eight it won't be my business. There's a pub three streets down, on the left, the Lion. I'll have telephoned my report by then.'

'It's a date. And I'll be buying the drinks.'

'Some of them,' Edward Heath said politely. 'Good luck with your future father-in-law.'

'You think I may need it?'

'I'm not paid to think.'

7

Mrs Miriam Meyer swept into the restaurant and Charles Russell rose at once to meet her. He was thinking the years had treated her kindly. She was fifty and if you looked hard showed it, but she was attractive still with her fine full figure, a worldly and distinguished woman. She had put on some weight above the elbows but it was evident had a very good masseuse, and she ate sensibly, which she proceeded to show. She wasn't on any fiddling diet but she went carefully with the carbohydrates. She chose steak with new peas but no potatoes, and though the sweet trolley would have broken most women, Brie cheese and a crispbread after it. The wine was for Russell and that was that. She was a woman who'd always known her own mind, and now in a vigorous middle age, the aura of Meyer's wealth around her, she could be imperious though never arrogant.

'What's all this I hear? This fantastic story?'

'I don't know till you tell me, do I?'

'You're older,' she said, 'but you haven't changed. You haven't altered a single bit.'

It was typical of Miriam Meyer that she hadn't wasted time in sparring. She had flown into London and telephoned Russell. He had asked her to lunch next day. Here they were.

He watched her demolish the steak with appetite. She had certainly put on a pound or two, Lester Meyer's wife had the right to do that, but they were judicious pounds and well controlled, she was miles from the steatophagous Jewess. For unmistakably she was now a Jewess. She hadn't been that when he'd known her before, just the barest hint from one of four grandparents, a sort of innocent but provocative bloom which had knocked young Captain Russell flat. Now he looked at her with a cool experience, thinking these genes were very strong. You could never escape and if wise didn't wish to. Miriam Meyer had clearly not wished to. She was married now to a man of her race, successful and properly proud of success, solid and friendly and quietly formidable. She wore a splendid ring with a single fine stone. Diamonds were one of her husband's interests.

She finished the steak and looked up at Charles Russell, the gesture exposing a single chin. 'I'm going to tell you a story, Charles, which I don't conceal is why I'm here. When I heard it I jumped the first aircraft there was. I more than suspect you've heard it too, but there's a point in my repeating it. I just want to be sure that we've got the same version.'

'That sounds sensible,' Charles Russell said. She had always had a disciplined mind.

She told him the story of Maurice Pater, up to but not beyond the framing, reciting it briefly but comprehensively, and at the end caught his eye and held it firmly. 'Is that how you have it too?'

'It is. May I ask how you learnt yourself?'

'From my daughter. Maurice rang her when those clowns broke in, and she and the man she was with went back to him. They very sensibly sent him to Harry Tuke, and since Charles Russell has this story too my guess is that Harry Tuke is his source. You were always as thick as the thieves you are.'

'You're an excellent guesser.' He drank some claret. 'All in the family so far—no damage. I can see how that could be rather important. But this man she was with——'

'Is called Pieter Brouwer and he works for my husband. Also he means to marry Barbara.' For a second she was an inch off stride, tolerance and what might almost be anger fighting a battle which tolerance won. 'I gather that they've been jumping the gun, but nowadays that's hardly eccentric.' She gave him a very adult smile. 'But the wedding will of course be white.'

'Naturally,' Charles Russell said. He watched her dispose

of the Brie, felt nostalgic. She had always used a knife like that, with firm sharp strokes which snapped through to the plate. 'So you jumped on an aircraft to talk to your daughter?'

'Not entirely that—there's Maurice too. Can I have coffee, please? And a brandy?'

Russell ordered both, lit her long cigarette. . . . What did Miriam Meyer now think of Pater? She was a generous and a warm-hearted woman, it was impossible that she'd ever borne malice. Besides, she had had no reason to, Pater had always been wholly correct. No doubt that was one of several reasons why an unpromising marriage had actually broken, but she had married him and she hadn't been innocent. He'd been a lawyer with a lawyer's virtues but also defects which were hard to live with. . . . Show me a valid precedent, show me the man with the better title. And of course he had disappointed her, for she'd been ambitious and unashamedly worldly. But Russell didn't believe she'd have left him solely because of material failure. Then what had she really felt when she'd gone? He didn't know that but he'd risk a guess. So contempt was too strong, irritation too weak. Perhaps the right word was simply pity. Maurice Pater had had his rectitude, his inflexible standards of right and wrong. A woman like Miriam might well feel pity but she wouldn't be able to live with it long. And what she was living with now was news, something she hadn't told him yet.

'I suspect you've got something to tell me,' he said.

'There's been an attempted but unsuccessful attack on Maurice.'

'I didn't know that.'

'Tuke didn't tell you?'

'Tuke asked me to help. I declined. Why should he?'

She told him about the Greek with the knife and Russell listened carefully. But a part of his mind had another problem. It was thinking about what was mostly called courage, conscious that as a verbal umbrella the word was both clumsy and imprecise. . . . You're a man who for all his working life has been treading the tightrope of sane opinion, and suddenly, no matter the motive, you see the flash in the sky, hear the roll of thunder. So down you go to the House of Commons and you speak the truth as at last you've seen it. Charles Russell would never have done it—never. It would have struck him as an excess of zeal, a compulsion to take decisive action which by habit must be firmly disciplined. On the other hand he'd been decorated and no man had ever been more surprised. He'd been battle-drunk, blind scared, blind angry, but when they'd hung it on him Charles Russell had sweated.

He returned to Miriam Meyer sharply. 'I can guess where that Edward Heath had been sent from and I can also guess who put it in gear. So he and your Pieter Brouwer *know*. Have they told Pater too?'

'They have not. They agreed between them that wouldn't be wise.'

'They agreed between them extremely wisely.' He looked at her quickly. 'Come to that, how do *you* know?'

'Pieter Brouwer rang my husband who pays him. He does business for Lester in London quite often.' She returned his inspection with steady dark eyes. 'An employer is entitled to know that a knife attack has been made on his servant.'

'I see,' Russell said, but he didn't precisely. There was something behind this and not his business. If Miriam meant to tell him she would and if she didn't he wouldn't extract it by questioning. In fact it was she who asked the next question.

'Will Tuke know of this?'

'I think so, certainly. The organization this Heath belongs to will have been instructed to act by Harry Tuke, so naturally they'll report any action.'

'I'm not happy,' she said.

'For Maurice Pater?'

For the first time she dropped her bold clear gaze. 'He was my husband and I bore his daughter. We had—well, there was affection once.'

He believed her without reservation since he knew she was a natural giver. He had taken her to Venice once, a young serving soldier without much money. She'd had that and had tactfully hinted at sharing but Russell had equally gently declined. When he took a lady away for ten days he preferred it in the old-fashioned manner. Now he was gratefully thinking it typical that she made no demands of emotion whatever, no appeal to the past either open or covert. They'd been to Venice together and both had profited. She didn't consider he owed her a thing beyond the claims of an established friendship.

And one of the pleasanter memories in a life which was fruitfully full of them. Russell saw that she still had the same broad shoulders, and her breathing was deep and exceptionally slow. Sometimes at night he had lain awake listening, for her sleep had been almost a conscious act, like a baby's, intense, a recharging of energy. And always there'd been that powerful breathing, the opulent bosom in swell and ebb. . . . What was the normal rate for a woman? But he hadn't brought Miriam Meyer to Venice to measure the night-rate of women's breathing. If he had she might now be demanding favours instead of talking in easy relaxation with a male with whom she had shared a success.

'Yes, it's Maurice who really worries me.'

'I don't see why now Tuke's taken a hand. Evidently he's efficiently guarded.'

'But a blasting out of a passing car——'

'I agree that's always on in theory, and in that sort of league you can do very little. But I don't think we are in that league just yet. It's one thing to try to injure a man, to put him out till he's no longer a nuisance, but public shooting in a public street is in a different and more ambitious class.'

She considered it over the second brandy, then asked an entirely masculine question. 'How good is this lot which is after Maurice?'

'Divided and mostly amateurish.' He smiled at her. 'Not a patch on your own.'

'But they'll have one or two good ones?'

'They all of them do.'

He was thinking that this was at best a half-truth. The truth was that a single good man was a match for any other who lived. A competent organization was better, but a determined agent who knew his job wasn't something to underestimate stupidly.

Miriam Meyer asked unexpectedly: 'Have you happened to hear of a man called Georges Bresse?'

'The name rings a bell from other days.'

'He's in London, you know.'

'No, I didn't know that. May I ask how you do?'

'My husband told Brouwer and Pieter told me.'

'*How did your husband know? Why tell Brouwer?*'

'No comment. I'm sorry but you'll have to accept it.'

'I'm sorry if I've been maladroit.' He considered it in the friendly silence, an ancient instinct stirring uneasily. . . . Georges Bresse—there'd been a file on that one. 'Listen,' he said finally, 'you haven't asked me for help and I'm grateful for that. Anyway, I couldn't have given it. For one thing I'm too old for games and for another the pros are involved already. But I'll very gladly talk to Brouwer if you think that it could possibly help.'

'I was playing for that one,' she told him coolly.

'I confess I didn't see it coming.' His laugh hid a very acute respect. 'I can see that you haven't lost your edge.'

'Tonight?' she asked.

'By all means. Send him. But tell me what sort of man he is.'

'He was a policeman once—Lester pulled him out. Now he's a sort of general factotum.'

'No comment,' Charles Russell said in turn.

'Quite so. Also he's an Afrikaner, and finally he's marrying Barbara. He was on his way to Maurice when he ran into that man with a knife, on his way to get Maurice's blessing to marry.'

'And did he?'

The question seemed to astonish her. 'Of course he did. Not that it would have made any difference if Maurice had been tiresome about it, but Maurice is above all things scrupulous and he'd never allow a dislike of South Africa to prejudice judgement about a South African. And that's what Piet Brouwer is, a real one. I'm much happier for Barbara than I was with that Beech-Lyon or whatever. So is Lester and that counts with me.'

'So Brouwer's an Afrikaner?'

'Emphatically. With a name like that what else could he be? But you won't be meeting a caricature.'

'I don't see the husband of Miriam Meyer employing a caricature as factotum. I think that was the word that you used.'

'Very prettily taken. Tonight then?'

'At seven.'

'And thank you, Charles.'

'Not at all. A pleasure.'

She got up and he went to the door with her. 'Miriam——'

'What is it, Charles?'

He took the hand with the single fine stone and held it.

'Thanks again,' she said. 'Don't say it. though.'

The studio was breathlessly quiet, that suspended instant before they went live which caught even the oldest hand by the throat and for Maurice Pater, a novice to telly, had an intensity which made him shiver. He was mildly surprised to be there at all for at first he'd been asked to be one of a panel and had declined when he'd learnt whom the other two were. To one he had had no objection at all, a man whom he knew was a hack but fair, but the other had made his hackles rise stiffly. It wasn't only the man's pretensions though these were indeed sufficiently sickening, but there was also his brutally ruthless technique, the sneer into the public eye, the cheap point and the shameless interruption. Maurice Pater believed that debate should be civilized—the case put, the case properly answered, the summary. He'd neither fancy nor talent for mannerless in-fighting and knew that to expose himself would be asking for a humiliation. So he'd regretfully but firmly declined.

Next day they'd rung back with another suggestion: would he come, state his views and be faded out, of course leaving the other two free to answer? This he had accepted gladly since if he put his case badly the fault would be his, not some oaf's whom no chairman or judge would tolerate, and he was more than ever convinced by now that the road to disaster lay through fudging the issues. And secretly he was also flattered. It was one thing to be asked to a panel, the tame M.P. whose views were known; it was another to rate special terms. Though he hadn't himself suggested it he knew this arrangement was far from usual. He wasn't a conceited man and he didn't believe this made him important, but he had more than enough experience to assess the concession for what it was worth. Which was that though he wasn't important yet he had certainly found a voice, a platform. Maurice Pater was suddenly controversial.

A make-up girl had powdered his bald patch, warning him not to drop his head. Now he sat in his chair in the sweaty studio, watching for the light to come on. When that turned red there'd be millions watching, by far the largest audience which Pater had ever dared to dream of. They hadn't given a list of the actual questions but had indicated the general line. That line had been fair, he'd at once agreed, and he wouldn't be interrupted or bullied since there was nobody there to break civilized rules. When they'd finished with Pater—six minutes, they'd said—they'd simply switch it to another studio. It was unusual but the occasion important. The People had a Right to Know. Or so they had said.

He had hidden a smile.

On the instant the light went red at last the interviewer slipped into gear. Tonight they were taking the Middle East and Maurice Pater's views on that were known, the more impressive, if he might properly say so, since it was also known he had recently changed them. He turned the better of two profiles to Pater. Now that the Six Day War was over what did he feel should be done to heal it?

Maurice Pater looked straight at the camera. 'Nothing.'

It was the least expected of all possible answers and for a second it shook the experienced compère. But he hadn't fought up to where he was without the buttress of a superb technique.

. . . Would Mr Pater care to elaborate?

Certainly.

Maurice Pater was relaxed by now, coming over, though he didn't know it, with a sincerity and a simple punch which the world's finest actors could seldom command.

Certainly, though it was basically simple. Here was a friendly if alien people under naked threat to destroy it utterly, and few of us in our secret hearts could have let that happen without deep shame. Equally, few of us wished for embroilment. In the event we'd been spared the appalling choice for this people had saved itself without us. Then rejoice but examine your consciences too. If we'd ever had rights to intervene we had lost them when we hadn't done so. Now we had no rights at all.

... But the future, some international action. Peace, the United Nations. ...

Words. If by international action was meant some action by the effective Powers, the Israelis were not a stupid people, they had gained a great deal but would trade it happily. One gain they would probably wish to keep, but the rest would be negotiable for what had always been wanted and fought for—security. Then leave them to negotiate. God knew they had won the right to do that.

... Negotiate directly?

Yes.

... Negotiate with defeated enemies?

Negotiate with enemies who had tried to destroy them and failed to do so. Does that sound so strange? Does that offend you?

... But surely the United Nations——?

Withdrew the handful of men which was lawfully there. Do you ask that a sane and virile people put its children's lives in such hands again?

... But I'm still not quite clear what you feel we should do.

We should do our best to hold the ring, use our veto in the Security Council to kill anything masquerading as compromise. The Resolutions in the other place we can afford to ignore and so can Israel.

... Isn't this putting the clock back?

Yes. And bitterly I regret it too. All my life I've supported peace and reason, but you cannot buy peace by backing aggressors, and even by the most cynical standards salvaging unsuccessful aggressors is inviting them to repeat their crime.

... You realize that there's another viewpoint?

I realize you've somebody here to put it.

. . . Then thank you, Mr Pater. Good night.

You mustn't misunderstand me, though. I'll do anything I can to help.

He walked back into the reception room where a man put a drink in his hand and grinned. 'Mr Pater,' he said, 'that came over bang on. Some people have it and some just haven't. I take the other side very strongly myself, but a second dose of that would shake me. I don't agree but it needed saying.'

Georges Bresse had made his call to Paris, but he hadn't, as he'd hoped he would, been given firm orders or any at all. He hadn't been too much distressed that his master had had to leave Paris hurriedly; in the sick shock of an unexpected defeat there would be urgent calls on his time elsewhere; but it had been a blow that there'd been no one in charge, no one prepared to give orders and stand by them. Bresse was still not quite inured to this, the endless shifts in the sands of policy and the nagging knowledge that giving firm orders was something to be ducked on principle. Not for the first time he felt exposed. He knew that he had two disparate enemies whilst most operators had only one. Most agents indeed had an ally, the 'firm', but Georges Bresse worked alone without organized backing, or sometimes, he had grimly thought, with backers who fought each other first. They were no match for the body they tried to oppose —in a different league, as Charles Russell had said. Bresse's loyalty was to his master alone and to the cause which still shakily stood behind him. It was enough because it had to be but it was anything but reassuring.

And he was running very short of money.

When Abdul Jawal had phoned again Georges Bresse had been something more than doubtful. They had parted in open hostility, but there'd been an overtone in the other's voice, almost a humility and certainly a renewed appeal.

Georges Bresse had agreed to meet once more and the Arab's approach had been quite unexpected. . . . He, Abdul Jawal, had not been clever, he had in fact misjudged it badly. Specifically he had misjudged Maurice Pater. The attempt to bribe him had been a miscalculation and the suggestion that the bribe be increased had been flogging a horse already dead. As for the plan to silence by force that had failed and ignominiously. Said Abdul Jawal must accept those facts. Between them they'd turned a potential ally into a bitter and openly dangerous enemy, and for his part in this calamity Said Abdul Jawal must express regret.

Georges Bresse had bowed but hidden disquiet. His hunch was that something worse was coming. These diplomats had the wildest ideas.

This one was moving smoothly now from apology to a straight appeal, an appeal in the name of their common cause. Maurice Pater was now an enemy, the more dangerous for his sudden conversion. They had plenty of enemies, mostly inevitable, enemies by race and instinct, but Pater was a Gentile and by reputation an impartial man. When such a one went on television with the sort of statement he'd made last night he was listened to as the others were not. No discounting, no writing down, no suspicion. Conviction had shone out of the screen. This was the truth as an honest man saw it.

Also it was unacceptably damaging.

Georges Bresse had agreed since he couldn't dissent. The impact of that six minutes of talk had been impressive and undeniably deadly. The newspapers which normally rode the fence had begun to wobble dangerously, and one which had never forgotten Suez had printed what so far it hadn't dared to, that the Israelis were Europeans or at least that their culture was European. The threat to destroy them affected us all as the siege of Vienna had touched us all. Clearly it was our duty to help them. That couldn't be escaped by words and all thanks were due to any man with the courage to show us the road to duty.

So Bresse nodded and waited, still far from at ease. The change in Said Abdul Jawal's manner had impressed but not entirely convinced. He was saying, treating Bresse as an equal:

'We've had personal differences, mostly my fault. I'm appealing to you to put them behind you.'

'You need me again?'

'We all of us need you. The whole cause needs you.'

In Arabic, Georges Bresse was thinking, it didn't sound entirely emetic. It was that sort of language, you talked that way. In French he'd have brought his breakfast up.

'How do you need me?'

'To fix Pater finally.'

Georges Bresse had got up from his chair at once. 'To kill him? You should have thought of that earlier.'

'Not at all. Please sit down.'

'But you talked about fixing him finally.'

'Quite. But there are more ways of fixing talkers than killing them. You needn't go anywhere near Maurice Pater.'

Georges Bresse with reluctance sat down again. No idea which would work could emerge from this clerk but he owed it to his master to listen.

It came out with a surprising clarity for Abdul Jawal had switched to French and even though he spoke it poorly something of its lucidity stuck. But at the end Georges Bresse shook his head with decision.

'Too many holes. It isn't on.'

'You disagree in principle? With the basic idea of taking a hostage?'

'Not at all—it's the best you've had by far. But if we snatch his daughter where do we hide her? Where do we hold her, for instance? Tell me.'

Abdul Jawal explained and Bresse listened. To his private

surprise the plan wasn't silly. Said Abdul Jawal was an amateur and Georges Bresse had expected some half-baked plot, something to fill half an hour on the telly. A criminal with the longest sentence which a British judge had ever inflicted had been smuggled out of the country in the false bottom of a Dormobile van, but that had been a springing from prison, whereas in this case the security forces were known to be on the alert already. You wouldn't export Miss Barbara Pater in the bottom of a Dormobile van nor hide her in a country cottage. But Abdul Jawal didn't plan to do either. In Bresse's world he was a dilettante but in another he was a pro, accredited; he was a professional diplomatist with the advantages which that status gave him. He was planning to use them—misuse them, rather. Bresse knew that this plan had worked elsewhere, not for long but for the time they needed.

'You mean that you'd hide her here?' he asked. 'Use this embassy and accept the risk?'

'Why not if you can get her to us? I know it's a risk but it's my turn to take one.'

Georges Bresse agreed but did not say so. 'But you can't hold her indefinitely, and when she comes out . . .'

'I promise you she won't know where she's been.' Said Abdul Jawal was quietly confident. 'You forget we have our own doctor here. There are drugs. . . .'

Perhaps if they'd been talking Arabic Georges Bresse would have turned it down out of hand. In French it seemed worth just one practical question.

'For how long?'

'I can't tell you that, it depends how things go. Perhaps if Russia and the United Nations——'

'You can write off the United Nations.'

'Then say long enough to bridge the crisis, to keep Pater silent for vital days. Then she's found on a seat in a London park—no knowledge of where she's been whatever. She'll remember that she's been kidnapped of course, but you'll be out of the country by then. Successful.'

'How do I get her here?'

'Car—and this.' He took a neat leather case from a drawer in his desk. 'It's charged,' he said, 'and it lasts an hour. After that it'll be for the doctor to handle her.'

'It's risky,' Bresse said.

'There's a great deal at stake. For all of us.'

'Let me think.'

Georges Bresse did so. To a man who had chosen Bresse's profession the plan had an established simplicity; it had worked in Algeria—why not in England? If Pater could be threatened through Barbara then Pater might be controlled and silenced. No doubt it would be decidedly risky but Bresse's life was an uninterrupted risk. . . . To burst into a young woman's flat which previous and not unpleasant experience suggested was almost certainly shared; to anaesthetize and bring her back to this embassy. . . . No, it wouldn't be easy, the odds were against it, but if by some chance it did succeed for the first time Georges Bresse felt confident that they'd hold a real rein on Pater's tongue. And there wasn't a doubt Maurice Pater was dangerous. He was a menace to everything Bresse was committed to.

He heard his own voice in a faint surprise. 'I can try but I don't guarantee success.'

'No man can do more and most would do less.' Back in Arabic it didn't sound quite so shame-making. 'When do you think you can start?'

'Tomorrow. There are one or two things I must find out first.'

'I've had a few of them looked into already.' A slip of paper came over, a self-satisfied smile. 'That's her address and the time she gets home. She shares with another young woman called Mary. Let me know at what time you want the car.'

'I will when I've looked over the ground. You'll have everything ready this end?'

'I promise.'

Georges Bresse would have rather he hadn't said it. A promise from a man like this was an omen he'd somehow contrive to break it.

As he went down the embassy steps he stopped, almost turning but deciding not to. He'd forgotten what really had made him come; he had almost no money and soon would need some. He hesitated but finally shrugged. He hated to ask for money from a man whom he still disliked and despised, and in any case he'd be going back. Oh yes, he'd be going back. With luck.

When Georges Bresse had gone the Arab laughed; he laughed till his fat shook, in near hysteria. He had decided he'd have to deal with Bresse, the impertinence was outstanding still, the insult unredeemed and festering. Bresse had swallowed the bait like a starving dog. How innocent these absurd Moors were, how ingenuous, how indecently trusting! After that scene a few days ago any Arab would have walked like Agag. But no, this half-Frenchman half barbarous Moor doesn't notice the trap and walks blindly in.

Said Abdul Jawal knew just how to spring it. Not the police—that would mean an unpleasant scandal—but that man he had met at a party once. His name was Charles Russell and everyone knew him. More accurately it was known what he'd done. He'd been head of the Executive and he was still a man of potent influence. He'd know exactly how to handle Bresse and the handling would be final too.

Said Abdul Jawal stopped laughing at last. He felt a man again, the scores would be even.

8

It was the third time they'd met in the Lion for a drink, for Edward Heath and Pieter Brouwer had discovered a taste for each other's company. It was the quick and not always surprising friendship of men from almost opposite backgrounds. Piet Brouwer found Heath entirely fascinating, the throwaway manner, the formal clothes, the air that you had to make it look easy even if you stayed sleepless all night swotting to get it perfectly right. Heath simply found Pieter Brouwer refreshing. Here was a man with roots, with beliefs. Some of them were preposterous but at least Pieter Brouwer held them sincerely. Fortunate Pieter Brouwer. Happy man. Each spoke to the other with shattering candour.

So after some drinks Heath was amiably insulting. 'Left your *sjambok* behind, I see,' he said.

'I don't carry it much in London, you know. Not that I haven't been tempted sometimes.'

'I know exactly what you're trying to tell me. All those terrible people——'

'I suspect you sometimes think I'm another.'

'I suspect that you're hiding behind that beard. There's another man there but I rather like him. You often talk really astonishing rubbish but I envy you the faith in it.'

'A drink on that?'

'I'll wait a bit, thank you.'

'Perhaps you're right, I've a date myself.'

'With your lady, no doubt.'

'No, a man called Charles Russell.'

Edward Heath put his glass down and whistled softly. 'You move,' he said, 'in exalted circles.'

'I don't move in any circles at all. My employers do and they take me with them.'

'Lester Meyer knows Charles Russell, then?'

'I don't think so but Miriam Meyer does. My guess is that she once knew him well.'

There was the comfortable silence of not too much alcohol. Heath said finally: 'I've seen Mrs Meyer. She must have been a dazzler once.'

'She's still a very exciting woman.'

'Who can send you to Charles Russell?'

'Why not? I've worked for her husband for several years.'

'Lester Meyer,' Heath said, 'must have many interests.'

Piet Brouwer had lowered several whiskies but in an instant was entirely sober. 'Many interests and one passionate cause.' He looked at Ted Heath very hard indeed. 'I thought you said you weren't a policeman.'

'I'm not, but you do come to London a lot.'

'You're asking directly?'

'No, nothing so crude.'

'But you're guessing?'

'Quite privately.'

'I can't stop you guessing.'

'You really don't have to. Not yet, at least. Don't press it too hard, though—that's always dangerous.'

'Then let's leave it like that and drink to it.'

'Later.'

Pieter smiled at Ted Heath. 'So you think I'm tight?'

'I can see you're not tight but you're meeting Charles Russell.'

'He can't eat me, man.'

'With that conscience of yours I wouldn't bet.'

Brouwer looked at his watch as he left the Lion for his appointment was at seven o'clock and he had still to get to Charles Russell's flat, and in another and grander part of London Said Abdul Jawal took his watch out too. Piet Brouwer had simply wished to be punctual but Said Abdul Jawal had a problem of time. Georges Bresse had rung to confirm his reconnaissance, and though Barbara got back about six o'clock Bresse intended to act a little later. It appeared that the English took baths after work and he couldn't abduct a naked girl.

Against his instincts the Arab had been impressed. This man knew his business, he really did. In some ways he almost regretted betraying him. 'What time should I send the car?' he asked.

'At eight.'

'And the key?'

'In the glove-box, please.'

'Understood. In the glove-box.'

'Not CD plates.'

'Of course no plates.'

'That's all, I think.'

'Very well. Good luck.'

'And everything at your own end ready.'

'I promised you that. Good luck again.'

Said Abdul Jawal watched the clock drag round slowly, then at half-past seven he picked up the telephone. He'd known no better moment in all his life. He was at peace with the world and at peace with himself. Above all things he was at peace with Georges Bresse.

He dialled and a man's voice answered crisply. 'Charles Russell, but I'm afraid I have company.'

'I'm sorry to interrupt you. I must.' He'd decided that an anonymous call would be ignored or possibly passed to the police, so gave his name and his rank and the name of his embassy. What was the difference? Georges Bresse would be finished. Then he began to talk fast and urgently.

Georges Bresse had simply rung and walked in, shutting the door behind him carefully. He didn't know the girl who had opened but there was another in an armchair, reading, and he'd seen photographs of Barbara Pater.

Georges Bresse looked round with a cool curiosity. He

had been in such rooms before and knew them. They were something more than temporary camps but somehow they were never homes. Two girls shared and were comfortable—that was all. The girl he had pushed past was talking, protesting, but Bresse hadn't the time to waste in chat. What he must do he hated doing but at least he could do it cleanly and clinically. He hit Mary just once with the side of his hand, catching her before she fell. Then he carried her to the sofa and turned.

Barbara hadn't screamed or moved. A good one, he thought, if her father wasn't. He walked over and stood above her, silent.

'There's nothing valuable in this flat,' she said.

There'd been contempt in her voice and a natural fear but there hadn't been even a shadow of panic. He took out the leather case and the hypo. It was loaded still but he checked it thoroughly. 'Don't struggle and you won't feel a thing.'

The fear in the eyes had deepened to terror, but as he felt for her forearm she stood up strongly.

'Stand still.'

'*You stand still.*'

It was a man's voice in authentic anger and Bresse swung at the sound on an instant reflex. He hadn't heard Pieter's key in the lock since Pieter had never meant him to hear it. What he saw was two men, one young, one older, and the younger was holding a silenced pistol. And it was evident he was used to firearms.

The older man spoke. 'Drop that thing at once.'

Georges Bresse dropped the hypo. It broke as it fell. Barbara said simply: 'Piet,' and was silent.

The older man was talking again. 'Miss Pater? Introductions later. For the moment move away to your right, out of the line of Pieter's fire.' He moved his head to look back at Georges Bresse but the man with the gun hadn't moved a muscle. Bresse could see that the weapon was no man's toy and it was covering his stomach squarely. He'd seen wounds in the stomach from forty-fives and they were wounds which he'd always wished to forget.

'Now up against the wall. And fast.'

Georges Bresse smiled politely.

'The wall, man. Move.'

Piet Brouwer had remarked to Heath that Charles Russell wouldn't be eating him, but would have confessed that he wasn't quite at ease. He'd been a policeman and not a senior one, and moreover he had something to hide. That something might not interest Russell since it damaged his country in no way whatever, and there were laws, made by States and mostly fiscal, which Russell was known to think simply silly. But the fact remained that Russell was Russell, an Olympian in his own dangerous world, whereas Piet was Piet Brouwer, a simple ex-policeman, a man of a culture different from Russell's and one which was often suspect wrongly.

But he needn't have felt any apprehension. Charles Russell was at ease with most men and with the younger he had a tried technique. He simply ignored the difference in ages, apparently unaware it existed; he neither patronized nor fished for respect. If the younger man had something to say Charles Russell would hear him out politely. If he found it of interest he'd listen till midnight.

Nevertheless Charles Russell's flat had shaken Pieter Brouwer considerably. He had never seen anything like it before. He had been in exceedingly plushy hotels and in the palaces of Johannesburg's magnates, and since Russell was known to be comfortably off he had expected a distinguished luxury. What he saw instead was a careless comfort, but the carelessness hid an instinctive taste. The furniture was of every period, a jumble but every piece belonged, and the rugs, he could see, were quite first class, not hung on the walls like museum pieces but thrown on the floor to be walked on cosily. There was a painting of a man in a ruff which Pieter couldn't begin to date, but the face was the face of another Charles Russell looking down with Charles Russell's urbane appraisal. Another was a *décolletée* woman, a Lely, he guessed, or at least of that period. A professional interior decorator would have wept at this room and wrung his hands: Pieter Brouwer, instead, made an instant decision. If he ever had money, a great deal of money, this was the sort of room he'd have.

'Can I offer you something to drink?'

'May I wait?'

'You won't mind if I do?'

'No, of course not.'

Charles Russell mixed a whisky, purring. He could see that Piet Brouwer had taken some drink, which was something he considered natural, but he'd shown he knew how to say no and gracefully, and Charles Russell approved that even more. Piet Brouwer, though he didn't know it, had started with a two holes lead.

'Mrs Meyer tells me you're marrying Barbara.'

'I suppose you could say that was premature. Up to a few hours ago I hadn't got her father's blessing.' Russell had succeeded perfectly: Piet Brouwer was entirely at ease.

'May I lean on a friendship with Miriam Meyer to ask if you obtained it easily?'

'More easily than I'd dared to hope. He objects to the *idea* of me, and from his point of view I can't say I blame him. But he's much too fair-minded to hold that against me.'

'And if he'd said no?'

'We'd have gone ahead—naturally. But I wouldn't have been quite happy to do it.' Piet looked at Charles Russell, respectful but firm. 'Parents,' Pieter Brouwer said, 'are important in the country I come from. Have you ever been to South Africa, sir?'

'Yes, I have. Several times.'

'I suppose it would be an impertinence to ask you what you thought of us.'

'It wouldn't be an impertinence but I'd be simply a fool if I answered you.'

'That's what Ted Heath always tells me too.'

'You've met him then?'

'Not the one you mean. Ted Heath is the chap they put on to guard Pater.'

'Yes, of course,' Russell said, 'so that brings us to business.'

They discussed it as equals, making sure that each man had the story the same. Finally Charles Russell summed up.

'So far it's been distinctly messy, but if we're right in our thinking of who's behind it, then a mess is what I'd expect to find.'

'Do you think Pater's perfectly safe now he's guarded?'

'No, I didn't say that.' Charles Russell smiled gently. 'I'm retired, you know, and I greatly enjoy it, but if I thought this affair was completely over you wouldn't be sitting where you are, not even at Miriam Meyer's suggestion.' He considered, but watching Brouwer closely, deciding the best play was straight down the middle. 'I know that you've heard of a man called Georges Bresse. I know because Mrs Meyer told me.'

'Yes, I know what he does and I know whom he does it for.'

'He's normally based in Paris, though. Would you care to guess why they switched him to London?'

'The obvious guess is to handle Pater, but the signs seem to be he was sent here on loan. Trying to bribe a man like Maurice Pater doesn't sound like Georges Bresse's idea a bit. He's half a European still and he'd know at once what was incorruptible, so if he played any part in that clumsy affair he was playing it under another man's orders. The business of those dirty pictures runs a good deal closer to Bresse's own form, but he'd never have stood for a Greek with a knife. I don't mean that he'd shrink from violence, but if he'd agreed he'd have gone himself.'

'I see you've been doing some homework on Bresse.'

'A little. I still have some useful friends at home.'

'And I a few connections here, whose opinion doesn't much differ from yours. May I offer you that drink again?'

'I'd enjoy it now. Thank you.'

As he mixed it unfussily Charles Russell was thinking. His conclusion would have astonished Brouwer, who'd been conditioned to think in black and white; he was accustomed to either being liked, liked as the pleasant young man he was, or to a bitter and unrelenting hatred based, or as often as not misbased, on what the hater supposed Pieter Brouwer stood for. Charles Russell was neither hating nor loving: what Russell felt was regretful envy. Not Piet's youth and his abundant health and certainly not the adventure of matrimony, but his roots and his unquestioning standards. Young Afrikaners, Israelis too, had something they really believed in, would fight for. Mistaken ideals? Charles Russell mostly thought they were, though the rabble which chanted loudest was suspect. Russell's mind shrank from judgement, he'd rather observe. So these splendid young men had their splendid ideals, or alternatively they were wicked racialists. Take your choice if you must at morality's level but accept what you saw at the level of life. These men had something to live for and did so. If Russell had ever had a son he'd have wished him quite other roots but as strong.

He returned with the whisky, brisk and practical. 'So we seem to agree about Georges Bresse.'

'But he's potentially pretty dangerous still. Will your friends pick him up?'

'Good heavens, no. I won't pretend Edward Heath's superiors run their business like lawyers scratching for evidence, but the political implications are frightening. There are several ways, all outside the law, of dealing with Bresse and with people like him, but in this case he has an edge on us and a part of that edge is your future father-in-law. If Maurice Pater learnt what was really happening, a private political battle in England, do you think he's the type to say nothing about it? I'm afraid that was a rhetorical question, so the answer is an emphatic no. Short of murdering Bresse, which he hasn't yet earned, we've no means of stopping his mouth and a scandal. And it *would* be a scandal, I tell you that. Moreover it wouldn't be only Pater who'd start raising a cloud of dust and protest. He's the one with the personal motive, true, but the great British public would kick as well. May I tell you what the public thinks about a war which doesn't directly affect it? It thinks a plague on both their alien houses. If the popular Press got hold of the story, fooling about with a British M.P., running what they'd call a spy ring—not a major one either, we're used to that— but the twopenny-ha'penny Mid-Eastern affair . . .' Charles Russell shook his handsome grey head. 'I had a Minister once called Harry Tuke and a tough old hand he was and is. If anyone did that to him by stupidly breaking the story open I don't think that man would last an hour.'

'I confess I hadn't thought of that.' Pieter looked at Charles Russell with growing respect. 'I can see how you earned your reputation.'

'That's kind of you but it isn't the point. The point is Georges Bresse and he's still in London.'

'You're not saying you couldn't get him out?'

'No, I'm not saying that—I'd very much like to. But so far he's a man in the shadows. We're sitting here talking; we suspect, we don't know. I'd like him to make a move—a wrong one.'

'But meanwhile Maurice Pater's safe?'

'I told you I couldn't be sure of that but it's not what

I'm really frightened of. In this trade, you see, you never know.'

The telephone rang and Russell answered it. 'Charles Russell,' he said, 'but I'm afraid I have company.'

Piet Brouwer could hear a voice talking urgently. He could hear no words but he watched Russell's face. It had been mildly annoyed at first, then incredulous. Now it was hard in the lines of decision. 'Very well,' he said, 'thank you.' He turned to Pieter. 'Do you carry a gun?'

'In London I wouldn't dream of it.'

'I'm rather afraid we're going to need one.' He unlocked a drawer quickly. 'Forty-five and stops most things. Here's the silencer too. Fit it on in the car.'

'Where are we going?'

'To Barbara's flat.'

'The wall, man. Move.'

Georges Bresse stood his ground and Charles Russell his, but he wasn't prepared to waste time in bluffing. He said to Piet Brouwer, not moving his head:

'How good are you with a pistol now?'

'Nothing fancy but they trained me once.'

'Then give him one just as close as you dare.'

There was the clunk of the silenced forty-five. The bullet went into the wall and stayed there. There was a spray of plaster, then total silence. Georges Bresse had moved back against the wall.

'Good,' Russell said, 'that removes a doubt.' Keeping carefully out of Piet Brouwer's sights he frisked Georges Bresse with casual competence. 'He's unarmed,' he said, 'but that doesn't surprise me.' He turned to Barbara Pater politely. 'I'm Charles Russell and a friend of your mother's. Now tell me what happened. Shortly, please.'

Barbara was still terrified but she saw that this wasn't the moment to break. 'Mary opened the door and this man pushed in. Then he went for Mary and knocked her out.'

Russell went to the sofa and looked at Mary. She was unconscious still but coming round, twitching and occasionally moaning. Russell felt her jaw, then her neck, and nodded. 'He knew his business—she's not hurt badly. And after he'd dealt with your friend, what then?'

'He came at me with that thing he had.'

'But he didn't have time to use it?'

'No.'

'Excellent,' Russell said. 'Now relax.'

He sat down himself in the second armchair. Pieter Brouwer was still covering Bresse. On the sofa Mary was muttering faintly. Russell spoke to the man by the wall. 'You're Georges Bresse, my name's Russell.' He was speaking French and he spoke it well.

'Honoured,' Bresse said.

'But I'm disgusted.'

'Permit me to remind you, my colonel, that we both of us have demanding trades.'

'I accept the point in principle but I do not accept what you planned to do.' He looked at the broken hypodermic, piecing the story together quickly. So Bresse had had no interest in Mary but had dealt with her as needs he must. But he did have an interest in Barbara Pater and had carried a hypo to block her out.

Or had it been only to block her out? There was a doubt here and Russell rose to check it. He picked up the hypo and smelt it suspiciously. Since he wasn't a chemist this told him nothing, except that it wasn't a well-known killer. Bresse said quietly: 'It wasn't a poison, you know.'

'Since I can't see a motive for common murder I'll accept what you so kindly tell me.' Charles Russell returned to his chair and thought. So Bresse had intended to drug the girl. Why? To search the flat? That was most improbable.

Nothing was known in this flat of interest, and in any case why bring a drug for a search? Why not deal with this girl as he'd dealt with the other? But if the intention had been a quick abduction . . .

He switched suddenly to his native English. 'Tell me where you were going to hide her.'

'You can't expect me to answer that.'

'No.' Russell said, 'I know I can't.' He was watching Georges Bresse with a steady stare but the stare hid a private and horrified pity. Charles Russell's voice went surprisingly soft. 'I see. Did many people know of this plan?'

Georges Bresse didn't answer and Russell went on. He'd been an interrogator of the highest class, which meant that his methods were highly personal. 'There's a question which you might reasonably ask me.'

'I'm asking no questions, my colonel.'

'Rightly. So I'll ask it of myself aloud.' Russell said on a note of rising inquiry: 'Now how does this colonel know that I'm here?' He was still watching Bresse and his eyes had flickered. On the sofa Mary moaned again faintly. Barbara and Pieter Brouwer were utterly and tensely silent. One was still feeling a little sick, the other was entirely fascinated.

'You can't trick me,' Bresse said.

'I don't need to trick you—I can see we're communicating. Obliquely, but we're communicating.' A thought struck him and he went to the window. 'I imagine you were expecting a car.'

No answer again but another flicker.

'Just for your information, Georges Bresse, there's no car outside and none in sight.'

The silence was oppressive now, Georges Bresse by the wall and Pieter still standing. Mary had opened her eyes and shifted. 'Go to her,' Russell told Barbara. 'Quietly.'

Georges Bresse had been standing rigid, fighting—fighting, Charles Russell knew, for control. It took him perhaps a minute to win it but he said at the end of the minute steadily:

'I should like to talk French again, please.'

'By all means.'

'What are you going to do with me?'

'Ah. . . . That's as much a question for you as for me.'

'But you hold all the cards.'

'You may think so—I don't. I've a wide choice of courses to deal with you, but short of a cold-blooded killing—I loathe them—I can't deprive you of the power of speech. And you carry a very embarrassing story. I've political friends whom that wouldn't suit, political friends who'd do much to avoid it.'

Georges Bresse thought it over. 'How much?' he asked.

'Would you give me a promise?'

'Very probably not.'

'No answer could reassure me more.' Charles Russell was as bland as cream. 'In point of fact I don't need your promise. You can leave for Paris—be out by midnight. If you're not out by then I'll have to act. Reluctantly but you'll force me to do it.'

'What's to stop me from talking in Paris?'

'Nothing. You can talk till you choke, it's all one to me. There'll be nobody here in arrest or detention, just a *canard* from a foreign source. An English editor would spike it on sight. He'd get little or nothing from Pater directly—for one thing he hasn't been told the whole tale and if he printed the story without hard evidence he'd have a writ round his ears first thing next morning.'

'You think of everything, my colonel.'

'Sometimes.'

Georges Bresse became suddenly very formal. 'Permit me to get this perfectly straight. I would wish to avoid any misunderstanding. It would offend me if you thought ill of me, or worse than I imagine you do.'

'I didn't say I thought ill of you. As you remarked your-self, we have our trades.'

Georges Bresse bowed stiffly 'Then you're letting me go?'

'You may leave this country perfectly freely provided you are out by midnight.'

'No other conditions?'

'I couldn't enforce one. Conditions which can't be enforced are meaningless.'

'*D'accord*,' Bresse said. 'Till we meet again.'

9

Harry Tuke looked round his splendid room, not quite at his ease but experience hid it. Too many people were present to please him, too many people who knew too much. He began to check them mentally, not happy still but in part reassured. It was a gathering of the clans, he thought, and the metaphor was mildly disturbing. He was tolerant of Gaelic whimsy, the great battles which had been border skirmishes, the great kings who had been grubby patriarchs, but they talked and talked and talked and talked. But this lot weren't Celts so they wouldn't chatter. He looked at them again and mellowed. Charles Russell was secure by profession and Brouwer was by blood a Dutchman, not a race to babble pointlessly nor a man to talk to boost his ego. Miriam Meyer looked a full-blooded Jewess. Tuke was wrong in this genetically but in every practical sense he was right. Her daughter would therefore have Jewish blood and both would know how to hold their tongues. So Charles Russell and a Dutchman and a Jewess and her half-Jewish daughter. It might have been worse, it might indeed. The important thing was Pater's absence. So far nobody had even commented and Tuke was quite confident nobody would. His absence hadn't been mentioned by anyone, it was something they silently took for granted. If you told Maurice Pater the frightening facts it was certain he'd somehow embarrass sane action. Which they were here to decide in collective wisdom. Harry Tuke was making that very clear. They weren't in this room to receive his *diktat*, which in any case would be quite unworkable if they didn't agree to play along. The disadvantages of publicity were so obvious he needn't state them, disadvantages to Her Majesty's Minister and much more than mere disadvantage to Pater. So Tuke had asked them to attend him today not only because of a Minister's interest; he was honestly anxious to pick their brains.

He was doing it very well indeed, using his Trade Union technique. He wasn't audibly calling them brothers and sisters but that was the aura he sought and exuded. They were here for consultation. Consult.

Charles Russell let the talk flow past him, thinking instead of the man Georges Bresse. He hadn't released him from senile sentiment. When he'd told Harry Tuke, Tuke had raised his eyebrows, but he'd taken the point as he always did and he'd taken the expected line: since he couldn't think of a real alternative objections would be academic; he didn't keep dogs and bark himself, only people like Maurice Pater did that. Charles Russell had let Bresse go—that was finished.

Georges Bresse, then—an exceptional man. He was a fool to have thrown it all up no doubt, his father's background and easy security; he was a fool but he wasn't a sordid one, nothing so wholly committed was sordid. Charles Russell would never have acted from sympathy, or never in any political matter, but he had always been on acceptable terms with his bitterest though professional enemies. He himself had a job which he liked and fulfilled him, but these others had something more, a faith. Charles Russell had always respected this and the others had sensed the respect and responded. So Georges Bresse had his faith and Charles Russell admired it. It was the Arab cause, whatever that meant, since when you tried to define it it fell to pieces. To Russell that was unimportant. Georges Bresse had caught the fever as a priest caught the fever of God knew what, and if he'd turned his back on his father's values he had won something else which might even be happiness. He worked for a third-rate organization, he'd been exposed, let down, and was now betrayed. None of these things would change his ideal. He knew what he wanted, Georges Bresse was content.

Harry Tuke was expounding and Russell listened. He was addressing himself to Miriam Meyer and Russell was in no way surprised. She didn't yet look like the classical matriarch but she was a woman who knew her own mind and spoke it. Miriam Meyer and the Minister Tuke had struck an immediate evident sympathy. 'The wedding . . .' he was saying now.

'Maurice will be coming out for it.'

'And after that?'

'I shall have to speak to my husband. You realize that.'

'Of course,' Tuke said smoothly, and Russell smiled. She still had affection for Maurice Pater, she had told him so without shame or regret, so she'd do for the man who had once been her husband what Miriam Meyer thought best for his interest. The fact that he might not think so too would be brushed aside with a good mother's firmness. As likely as not she'd act first, then tell him.

So happy Maurice Pater too, fortunate though he might not think so.

Russell began to doze unashamedly. He could seldom sleep much after seven o'clock and he liked, after luncheon, to get his feet up. Today he had lunched at his club and enjoyed it, cold pie and a salad, a carafe of claret. It wasn't a club for fussy eating but the cold table was the best in London. And he'd allowed himself a large vintage port. So he dozed and he dreamed and the dream made him smile. He was seeing it now, in wine's civilized haze, a story he'd heard in the bar that morning. Mussolini had gone to the Vatican to sign that absurd Concordat of his and naturally he'd been bull-frogging noisily. 'This will last,' he had said, 'for a thousand years, for as long as the Fascist State will last.'

'My son, I fear you are much mistaken.'

'Not a thousand years?'

'Not a tenth of that.'

The bull-frog had been somewhat put out, but also he was a good Italian. 'Then tell me, Holy Father, what will.'

'Certainly. First the Catholic Church.'

'Just so, Holy Father. That goes without saying.'

'Then the Standard Oil Company of New Jersey.' A shrewd and very Italian smile. 'In which I have an enormous holding.'

'And the third, Holy Father?'

'The Jewish people.'

Charles Russell awoke with a start, mildly shaken. To Russell, a protestant Anglo-Irishman, the Holy Father was the Bishop of Rome. But he had woken not from conscience but from hearing his own name spoken sharply. Harry Tuke was not a malicious man but there'd been something in his voice not quite amiable. 'Charles Russell,' he was telling Miriam, 'might help you with Maurice Pater in Africa.'

'I don't really believe you think he would.'

Diplomatically Russell dozed off again, or at least he feigned a post-luncheon snooze. In fact he was alert and thinking. If Miriam hadn't been what she was she might indeed have asked for Charles Russell's help, baiting the hook with the things he relished, a beautiful house, good golf and the climate. He might even have been gently tempted but not tempted enough to shake decision. A look at his diary would have promptly confirmed it. Next week would be fairly typical, two days' golf and that play he had still to see, not some complex if significant puzzle (and what did the adjective mean in any case?) but a straightforward experienced craftsman's job with an ending which left you moved and satisfied. *Katharsis*—that was really essential. Then on Thursday he had a little party, six people to dinner, not too old, not too young. They'd talk of anything and everything except the newly-praised novels they'd none of them read, the difficult concerts of modern music which they'd admit they had tried but had happily failed with. It would be absurd to throw all this up for Johannesburg, a city he found intensely stimulating but not one where he'd wish to live for long. Besides, the idea would be misconceived, as Tuke's own request for help had been fallacy. Charles Russell was sixty, not young any more, and though the tentacles which he still controlled included one which could easily reach to Pretoria it was by no means the strongest and not the most personal. Once or twice it had twitched but nothing more. What was wanted was not a ripe experience but some bright young man like Pieter Brouwer. After all, Lester Meyer was known to employ him.

Russell began to listen carefully, to the developing duel between Tuke and Miriam. They were down to the facts now and Tuke was leading.

'So Pater will go for the wedding?'

'Of course.'

'He'll be safe in Jo'burg.'

Russell winced at the 'Jo'burg' but went on listening.

'I'd like you to tell me why you think so.'

'Certainly, though it seems fairly clear. Any danger he's in he's invited by talking. Leaving aside the attempt to bribe him and the other attempt to force his support, he's now come strongly down on the other side. Too strongly to please the first—much too strongly. In his way he's increasingly influential, which to them means he's also increasingly dangerous.'

'But he wouldn't be in South Africa?'

'No.'

'Tell me why not again.'

Harry Tuke smiled. 'I think, Mrs Meyer, you know very well. Talking is one thing but hearing another. In England he's a Member of Parliament with a fine reputation and a ready-made platform. In South Africa he'll be just an Englishman, a man without any political influence. Here he writes for a week-end paper too but you don't have that sort in your own great country, and between ourselves I'll admit I envy you.'

'Good,' she said coolly, 'that clears up one thing.'

Harry Tuke made his next pass with growing confidence;

he clearly thought highly of Miriam Meyer. 'But there's also another factor. Time.'

'You mean how long till this affair blows over? How long till it doesn't really matter what Maurice says or anyone else?'

'I can't tell you that.'

'I feared you'd say so.' Miriam Meyer was silent, considering. 'So while the heat stays on there could still be danger?'

'In theory I'm obliged to admit it, but I wouldn't have thought you were wholly helpless.' Tuke looked at Pieter Brouwer deliberately. 'I understand Mr Brouwer now works for your husband.'

She began to laugh, not attempting to hide it. 'You're not as clever as I thought you were.'

He wasn't offended. 'Please tell me why.'

'We're Jews, you know—I believe you'd forgotten. Pieter's marrying into the family, which is one way of saying he'll be changing his job.'

'I see,' Tuke said, 'I'm afraid I was innocent.' He had finished his fencing, he had the facts, and he began to tick them off methodically. 'So Maurice Pater will go for his daughter's wedding. A week, would you say, or maybe a fortnight?'

'Which naturally I shall try to extend.'

'Just so, we're agreed.' Harry Tuke thought it over. 'I suppose there's no help I can possibly offer?'

'It's a very kind thought but I hardly think so. My husband has his own connections, and I don't mean a future son-in-law.'

'I understand that.'

'You're understanding.' Miriam Meyer rose, robust but graceful. 'I'm very grateful for this talk,' she said.

'It's been a pleasure. I really mean a pleasure.'

They filed out of the office and went down in the lift, standing in a group in the hall while the porter called Miriam

Meyer's car. Russell had guessed she had something to say to him and also that she would say it reluctantly, but Tuke had given her an opening which she would never have tried to make for herself.

'Since Tuke was the one to suggest it, not me . . .'

'That idea of his I might somehow help you? But I wouldn't in fact be the slightest use.'

'I disagree with that and so does Lester.'

'You flatter me but you've got it wrong. And you told Tuke yourself you had other connections.'

'They're not Charles Russells.'

'Lucky connections.'

'But you'll come to the wedding?'

'It's a very long way.'

'Still, I'll send you a card.'

'Which I'll decently answer.'

In his taxi he sat back smiling contentedly. Only one thought disturbed his euphoria, a thought for Maurice Pater, not himself. Miriam had some plan for Pater and it might not be one which he'd make for himself. But she wouldn't consider that for a moment, she'd sweep it aside as of no importance. He was a child in Miriam Meyer's world, a child to whom elders owed protection. Mother knows best and he couldn't escape it. One day, perhaps, he'd be properly grateful, but at first he'd be simply resentful and bitter.

Maurice Pater had been thinking hard, for he'd been delaying to do what he knew he must. More than he knew had in fact been happening, even so life had moved much too fast for reflection. He still had twenty thousand pounds which, though innocently, he had formally signed for. This he'd told Harry Tuke with the rest but Tuke hadn't offered practical comment. Presumably he had simply thought that a lawyer could deal with a legal matter, and perhaps he had been right at that. Tuke had resources, extremely formidable, but they weren't the resources of legal nicety.

Maurice Pater began to think as a lawyer though this wasn't entirely a lawyer's problem. But one lawyer's habit stayed him strongly, welcome because it was something familiar. He went to his desk and began to write.

1. Unless or until I convert this money I am demonstrably innocent.

2. Unless or until I get rid of it I shall demonstrably be under suspicion.

He nodded approval, that could hardly be bettered. It was succinct and a judge would have liked it. Alas that the last thing he wanted was judgement: what he sought was to avoid a smear. They'd been clever too, he'd signed his name.... In ignorance of what was inside the parcel? There'd be sniggers, quickly suppressed, in court, or more likely in some Commission's chamber. That wasn't the way to escape the trap. He took his pen and wrote again.

ALTERNATIVES

(a) To return this money is theoretically possible but also it would be quite unfruitful. I am morally certain it came from Saccone, but Saccone would of course deny it. He might even have a cause for action on the suggestion that he had tried to bribe me. In any case the last thing he'd do would be to give me a good discharge for it.

(b) To keep it here would be very dangerous and to put it in my bank quite fatal. Even in a special account.

(c) But I can't simply burn it or throw it into the Thames from a bridge. There is evidence I have received the money, there must therefore be even better evidence that I have dealt with it in a proper manner. And that evidence must be quite unchallengable.

He re-read this admirable summary carefully, then

settled to the real problem of action. In this he was on shakier ground for he'd never claimed virtues as man of affairs. A crime had been committed and a Member of Parliament gravely embarrassed. A felony or just misdemeanour? He'd never been much of a criminal lawyer, disliking the dust of the criminal courts, so he settled for simple 'crime' and left it. What was important was less what was past than the need for immediate action to meet it. No court would convict, he was certain of that, but a Member's reputation and future could be broken to pieces outside the courts. The strange looks and the averted eyes. . . .

He couldn't face those, not even innocent.

That was all very well, but what to do? Banks were out of the question, he'd few close friends. He had a daughter but she was now engaged and to embroil her would be gravely unfair. In the end he put the bills in a suitcase, taking a bus to his solicitor's office. He had considered a taxi but turned it down, partly because he was watchful of shillings and partly because of a prick of conscience that a man who couldn't dowry a daughter had no business to be taking taxis. He sat in the bus and nursed the suitcase, worried and more than a little uncertain. His solicitor had been Miriam's too and he'd sometimes sent him briefs though not many, but it was a very eminent firm indeed and careful of its proper standing. Pater couldn't consider this man a friend. Also, he remembered now, his solicitor was proudly Jewish. There were overtones there but their note uncertain. Since Pater must tell the whole story or none it might well engage a good Jew's sympathies, but he might also see shadows he didn't welcome and they were a cautious people as well as warm-hearted. Maurice Pater had learnt that fact from Miriam. Like Russell he knew these were very strong genes.

He told his story straight, though embarrassed, and the eminent solicitor sighed. 'I've heard of those ploys before,' he said, 'but never against a Member of Parliament.'

'You've been asked to advise on them?'

'Yes, I have. But it was a very different world from yours—much easier to advise it usefully.'

'Harry Tuke was against the police.'

'Understandably. In principle no doubt you should tell them but I don't see what the police could do. Sending you money is most suspicious, forgetting the other regrettable happening, but it wouldn't establish corruption in court. This *is* corruption—we both know that—but there's no evidence but what you've told me. And the police might not take the money off you.'

'I've got to dispose of it—that's essential.' Maurice Pater drew a long breath and shot it. 'I want you to take this money and hold it.'

The solicitor had expected this, he had noticed the suitcase and Pater's distress, but he hadn't made his mind up yet and there were evident and serious snags. Moreover, as Pater had thought, he was cautious. 'That might be conversion,' he said at length.

'I don't think so.'

'You don't?' The solicitor looked at Maurice Pater. 'Is that your advice to me as Counsel?'

'No, I'm not giving advice, I'm asking it.'

'I'm glad of that—I could hardly have taken it.' The solicitor considered again. 'A trust?' he suggested. He knew perfectly well there couldn't be one, but he still wanted time to think and was making it.

'A trust without a beneficiary?'

'You're perfectly right about that, of course.' The question had been a formality: as lawyers they had both known the answer. 'May I ask what you're really suggesting then?'

'I simply want you to hold that money.'

'To your order? On a proper receipt? But of course—nothing simpler.'

Maurice Pater dropped unhappy eyes. 'I'm afraid that

would hardly do,' he said. 'I have to get rid of this money somehow, and if there's a future complication I must be seen to have kept no strings on it.'

'But you must know that that's extremely irregular. Of course I don't believe you stole it but I've only what you tell me that you didn't do exactly that. In which case I'd be a common receiver.' He was still playing for time but had almost decided.

Maurice Pater made an attempt at firmness. 'I'm aware that this isn't normal business, but nor is the story which set it in train.'

The solicitor was a serious man but he allowed himself a sudden laugh. 'Even from an Englishman that's the litotes of the century.' He had made up his mind now, he'd help this man. Perhaps he was stiff and a shade too correct but you couldn't say Maurice Pater was smug. It wouldn't be improper, though, to suggest he was sometimes conscious of rectitude, but rightly so, that was what he had, and if this virtue could sometimes be mildly tiresome it was never contemptible, never cheap. What was more Maurice Pater was in a jam and the solicitor knew who had put him there. He knew the motive too and it wasn't pretty. Maurice Pater had been right in one thing. The solicitor was a Jew and proud of it.

'Though you haven't used the word yourself, what you really need is simply cover. Just depositing money here won't give it, any more than a special account in a bank would. It would be something in that direction perhaps, but it wouldn't be the discharge you want. With a receipt from me and held to your order it could always be said you were merely stalling, intending to return in time for money which you could still take freely.' The solicitor fell into thought again. 'You will realize what this implies,' he said. 'If I do as you ask it's not merely irregular, it means I could skip with the money myself. I could skip to Mexico City tomorrow.'

'I hardly think you'll do that,' Pater said. He said it with an unmoving face.

The solicitor smiled but not a wide one. He supposed that this man had a sense of humour but to a Jew it seemed a very blunt one. 'Then give me that suitcase, I'll have it locked up.' He rose and held a hand out. 'One thing. How long will your, well, your embarrassment last?'

Peter hadn't thought of that and hesitated. Finally he told the truth. 'I don't know that.'

'But I beg you—be reasonable. I'm accepting hot money—I think that's the term. You cannot expect me to hold it for ever. From anyone but respected Counsel I wouldn't have even looked at it.'

This wasn't entirely true but partly. Maurice Pater was a barrister but also he was a Member of Parliament. The solicitor had important clients and one could never be sure when a Member of Parliament mightn't somehow contrive to grease a wheel. This hadn't been a major motive, a genuine sympathy drove him first, but the factor was there and not one to ignore. He'd call it potential capital asset.

He hid a smile; he was fooling himself. Maurice Pater was in trouble and it was evident who had put him there. An enemy hath done this thing and the enemy was one in common.

Maurice Pater was standing, still undecided, and the solicitor showed a sharp irritation. 'You must realize that I'm accepting a risk. To be frank with you it's not a huge one, but if anything goes wrong for you then inevitably I'll be dragged in too. I could very probably talk my way out but a firm like this should avoid that necessity.'

'It's really very good of you.'

'Perhaps. But not *that* good.' He had dropped his hand but again held it out. 'Say three weeks,' he said, 'I hope that will suit you. You must settle this matter in twenty-one days, give me instructions for payment—to whom and how.

Failing that I shall feel perfectly free, and since ambiguity here is out of place that means I shall find one way or another to put the money back with you. Fair enough?'

'It's severe,' Pater said, 'but it's perfectly fair. I must thank you and I sincerely do so.'

He picked up his hat but he left the suitcase.

10

Georges Bresse left the flat grim-faced and resolute. As Russell had said there was no car outside, but Bresse hadn't needed this final warning to tell him what in fact had happened. Russell's word had been communicating and indeed the message had come across perfectly. Georges Bresse had been betrayed again and with him the cause he'd elected to serve.

He looked at his watch for time was important. He had given Charles Russell no promise at all, but nor had he even a second of doubt that if he wasn't away by midnight they'd take him. It was nearly nine so that gave him three hours. Three hours to do what he must, his duty.

He was more angry than he had ever been, humiliated and cruelly ashamed. What they said was quite true, the bitter jibe: whoever has Arab for friend needs no enemy. Through the shamed fury which the sneer begat he forced himself to think coolly and fast. Said Abdul Jawal would have left his embassy for he wouldn't have been expecting Bresse. No indeed he would not, he'd have quietly gone home, and if he hadn't Georges Bresse would wait for him. If he waited too long he'd run over his time, in which case Charles Russell would surely act, but that was the lesser risk by far. The greater was letting this evil thing live.

He knew the address and hailed a cab. It was a block of rather pretentious flats, manned by day by a porter but not at night, and Said Abdul Jawal mostly lived alone. At night the outer door would be shut and if Bresse rang it was certain he wouldn't gain entry, but it was a biggish block, there'd be constant movement, so he'd simply wait for a man with a key. In fact it was a woman and she was opening as he paid off the taxi. He slipped in with her with a neighbour's smile. The woman went into a ground-floor flat and Georges Bresse in the lift to the fourth and got out. He knew exactly what he intended to do and banged peremptorily on Abdul Jawal's door. He could manage the London whine quite well and in it he called: 'It's the police, the law.' It didn't strike him as extravagant. It was true that he was no sort of policeman but indubitably he was the law. He was the law of his race and the cause he served.

The door opened on Abdul Jawal in a dressing-gown. Bresse put a foot in the door, a hand in the face. He pushed the door and he pushed the face. The Arab went backwards and Georges Bresse in. Then he shut the door behind him carefully. 'Sit down,' he said, 'and listen. Don't move.'

He had weighed the priorities, worked to them scrupulously. First there was money, he needed that. If he had to he could break simple safes but he hadn't the time for complications.

'First give me money,' he said. 'Then we'll talk.'

Said Abdul Jawal had collapsed in a chair, huddled and shaking, plainly terrified. Georges Bresse had foreseen what he'd try to do: he started to chatter, to try to bluff it.

'Why have you come here? I said the embassy. I waited for you there——'

'You did not.'

'I don't know what you mean.'

'But you do. Not that it's important now. The money and be quick with it.'

Said Abdul Jawal got up unsteadily; he went to a wall safe and spun the dial; he came back with a bundle of ten-pound notes.

'That's all I have.' He was speaking the truth. Georges Bresse could see it and didn't doubt him. Said Abdul Jawal was too frightened to lie, which meant he was very frightened indeed.

Bresse counted the notes—a thousand pounds. It was more than he'd ever held in his life. . . . These shameless disgusting oil-sick *rentiers*. . . . He needed perhaps a couple of hundred, and the rest he'd just give to his master in Paris. 'Good,' he said finally. 'Now to business.'

Bresse could see that Abdul Jawal was broken but he'd steeled himself against pangs of pity. He rapped the question out like an old-fashioned drill pig.

'Have you ever met a man called Charles Russell?'

'I've heard of him but so have most people.'

'Have you recently been in touch with him?'

'No.'

Georges Bresse had been watching the other intently and the shifting eyes had confirmed what he knew.

He'd begun to move when the diplomat pulled it, a toy, Bresse could see, but a gun just the same. In the hand of a man who knew how to use them these two-twos could be as lethal as cannon but Bresse didn't believe this clerk was one of them. He came on steadily and the Arab fired.

He caught Bresse in the forearm but didn't check him. The other arm knocked the gun from his hand and both Bresse's went round the fattening neck. Maurice Pater had thought once how strong they were. When they let go Abdul Jawal was dead.

Georges Bresse stepped back and thought again. The pistol might have been heard or might not—in a matter of minutes he'd know for certain. He counted five of them but nobody knocked, so he looked at his watch again—half-past nine. There was a flight at ten but he wouldn't make that for he now had to do what he hadn't expected.

He took a taxi again to his single room, then pulled off his coat and rolled up his shirtsleeve. He knew that the arm wasn't broken—he'd used it—but also that he still carried the bullet. Georges Bresse smiled wryly. In his way he'd been something more than lucky. Twice in an evening men had pulled guns on him and the first, if it had hit an arm, would have pulped it and left it hanging useless. That woman's toy had left only the entry wound, a slug which had hit the bone and stuck.

So he'd been lucky but not as lucky as that. He didn't suppose that Abdul Jawal was a man who sterilized casual bullets and there was one thing which he feared more than torture, the gangrenous wounds which he'd seen in Algeria. Even in dreams they could still make him vomit.

He washed the wound while he made up his mind, but he knew all the time what lay before him. That is, if he could make himself do it and courage was known to be something expendable. Torture he'd suffered because he must, but it was pain which another man inflicted. Pain on yourself was entirely different. He wasn't sure he could do it, he knew he must. The horror of poisoned wounds had gripped him.

He had a pair of electrician's pliers, snipe-nosed and with luck just long enough, and a bottle of household disinfectant. He washed the pliers carefully, then he set his teeth and said a prayer. The first time he flinched, the second he fainted. When he came round he was wet with sweat. He cursed but he made himself try again. This time he reached it but only just. He tied up the wound, put the arm in a sling. He was now in very great pain indeed and he had still to make the morning flight.

At the airport he walked to the booking desk, noticing it was ten to midnight, and a stranger tapped his shoulder lightly.

'You're running it rather fine, my friend.'

Bresse was more scared he'd collapse in delirium than he was of some man who'd been sent to watch him. He fought his pain and said slowly but strongly:

'I know the terms and I'm sorry I've broken them. I'm afraid I've missed the ten o'clock plane but there's a flight at eight and I mean to take it. You can stay and see me off if you wish.'

'That won't be necessary.'

'Why? You trust me?'

'I'd be a fool if I did, Monsieur Bresse—I don't have to. The last scheduled plane was at ten o'clock and by the agreement you should have been safely on it. But there's been more than the usual airways muddle and they've put on another for one in the morning.' Heath held out a ticket. 'I bought this in case.'

'That was really very thoughtful indeed.'

'My employers are really thoughtful people.' Ted Heath looked at Bresse's arm in a sling. 'An accident?' he inquired politely.

'You could call it that.'

'Then so I shall.' Heath stared at the arm and suddenly frowned. Up to this he'd been quietly returning ironies but unexpectedly he was now a colleague. 'You've been wounded,' he said. 'Would a brandy help?'

'You're very kind.'

'My strict interest is to see your back. I shall report that I saw off a wounded man but I've no orders to ask you tiresome questions.'

'I had a job to do.'

'I can see you did it.'

In Paris Bresse drove to a woman's house, leaving the taxi two streets away. He found he could walk still but not very steadily. It was three in the morning, dead dark and raining. Georges Bresse was shivering, almost gone.

He had rung three times before she opened, but this time he didn't push past as she did it. She might somehow be hot and Georges Bresse was careful. The woman said: 'Georges,' and Georges Bresse said: 'Marie.'

'Where's the *patron*?' he asked. They called him that. It was a good French word and they always used it.

'He had to leave Paris—we told you that.'

'When is he coming back?'

'I don't know.' She put up a hand, not forbidding—

regretful. 'I can't take you in, I simply don't dare to. There was a drag last week and they picked up Francis.'

'I quite understand.' He turned but staggered. The woman spun him and caught his final fall. 'Very well,' she said softly, 'so I'm stuck with Georges Bresse.'

11

It had been half-past nine on a Friday evening when Georges Bresse had done what he'd known was his duty, but Said Abdul Jawal wasn't found till Monday, by the woman who came to do his cleaning. Russell saw it in the evening paper— DIPLOMAT FOUND DEAD IN FLAT—and the name was the name of the man who had rung him.

He considered the news with a rising distress, a foreboding that somehow events had trapped him. It didn't distress him this man was dead. It was certain that he had earned his death, and in the world which Charles Russell had learnt to accept that death had been invited and ran close to the inevitable. But Russell hadn't expected an immediate killing, certainly not a killing in England, so he'd rung to the Executive with a simple request which they'd quietly agreed to. He was interested in a man called Georges Bresse but provided he left the country by midnight that was the end of Charles Russell's interest. They had telephoned back on Saturday morning—Georges Bresse had been late but was duly out. They had added that he'd seemed in great pain, his arm in a sling and at moments light-headed. Since they'd had no instructions which covered this they had played it by Russell's and let him leave. Russell had said they'd done rightly and thanked them. Now he was in a dilemma of conscience.

He turned on the evening news and listened. At the moment there wasn't a great deal for headlines but the murder of a diplomat was something which the Press had pounced on. It was clear that the police would have liked to be cagey, but the biggest guns had been swung on them and they'd handed out the minimum, which the inquest would soon establish anyway. The charwoman had been talking wildly, a story of finding a strangled man, but that wasn't correct, he hadn't been strangled. His neck had been broken cleanly, professionally. And she'd talked about finding a gun—that was true. There was a gun on the floor and one round had been fired. No bullet had so far been found in the room.

. . . Of course not, Georges Bresse had that round in his arm.

Russell settled to think in increasing unease. Tell the police what he knew, the whole story? Dangerous. As head of the Executive he'd known of killings and kept discreetly silent, but he wasn't that now, he was Citizen Russell, but whose background, inescapably, was a background of the highest policy, of secrets, of friends like Harry Tuke. He owed him consideration at least, he couldn't ditch him by blowing a scandal callously. And nor would he tell the police half a story, even if he'd thought them so stupid that they wouldn't nose out the rest of it. Finally Bresse was now out of England. Even if he'd left evidence, and Russell felt fairly sure he hadn't, it was a very long bet that they'd never catch him. He'd slip back into the world of shadows from which he'd been sent to work in England.

Russell sighed into his drink, unhappy. He had let Bresse go because he must, seeing no alternative when it was politics, not a view of the law, which was determining a minimal choice; and if he'd done more than merely hint that he'd arrived at Barbara Pater's flat as a result of information received, that was something which Bresse had been certain to guess, and moreover he'd know who had shared in his plan and had therefore possessed the means to betray him. Russell had mentioned no names—Bresse had known.

Charles Russell began to feel rather less rueful. A dilemma of conscience? The phrase was inflated. He'd done nothing wrong and nothing wicked, even if he'd owned a mind which moved easily in terms of morals. What he'd done had been to make a mistake, not his fault on what he'd known at the time, but in the event quite a critical error of judgement.

And that was much more serious than some action which men like Pater might question. So he'd made a mistake and that was unfortunate but he certainly couldn't accept another. He owed that not to some abstract idea but to the private pride of a man called Charles Russell.

He started to make some regretted phone calls, checking them with his diary carefully. He cancelled two days of golf, a theatre; then he rang to six friends, not too young, not too old, and explained that he'd have to postpone their dinner. On his mantelshelf was the card from Miriam—*Mr and Mrs Lester Meyer request the pleasure of Colonel Charles Russell's company at the marriage of Miss Barbara Pater*. . . . It had been delivered by hand and he'd answered already—Colonel Charles Russell much regretted . . . Now he telephoned a telegram since Miriam had flown out on the Sunday. If he might he would like to attend after all. He'd explain on arrival if explanations were necessary. Finally he rang his travel agency, one in Ropemaker Street which knew him well. They were efficient, unfussy and used to Charles Russell. He'd be leaving tomorrow, by air of course, and he'd like to be booked at the Sunnyside Park.

No trouble at all, they'd cable at once. The air ticket would be delivered next morning. A pleasant flight and a pleasant stay. Short notice? By no means. We thank you as usual.

Decision made, Charles Russell relaxed, aware, if not of a state of grace, of a growing excitement he welcomed happily. He'd told Harry Tuke that he wouldn't come in, he'd told Miriam Meyer the same dull story. Now he'd dropped himself in and he couldn't escape it, not in good conscience and that was important. . . . Conscience again? The word was still suspect. He had one but it was admirably disciplined, so call it a sense of obligation. To Pater who'd been put under pressure, then made dangerous and revengeful enemies. It was true that in South Africa it would be twice as hard to do him mischief, but Russell, for sound political reasons, had released Georges Bresse who'd walked straight to a killing. He remembered again what he hadn't told Miriam, that a single good man was a match for anyone. If this wasn't an obligation what was?

He smiled into his third evening whisky. For even 'obligation' was in a private sense close to self-deception. . . . Maurice Pater, a painfully honest man, being bribed and then blackmailed to run a line. Lester Meyer who ran the opposite hard. His wife who had once been Pater's too. Pieter Brouwer who worked for Lester Meyer, though what he worked at was something less than explicit.

Once Russell would have been gravely tempted but now, he'd told Tuke, he wasn't interested; he simply wanted his golf and his fishing. That had been true at the time—not now. He'd gone stumbling in but he wasn't complaining. Old habits died hard and not always certainly; the old Adam never died at all. Though he hadn't planned to do any such thing Charles Russell had fallen in again, and to pretend that he didn't relish it would be the sin which he privately thought the worst, a sham, self-deception, a matter for shame.

He had never been a part of bureaucracy but in a matter of any real importance he liked to get it down on paper. This he did now and re-read it carefully.

1. Nobody can seriously suppose that Israel runs a major war by selling oranges to British housewives. Her sinews are in New York and London, in Paris and in Johannesburg too.

2. Equally, no one who knows the world can suppose that every penny she garners comes across to her on the open exchanges. Some certainly do but the rest will not, especially what comes from controlled economies.

3. Lester Meyer is wealthy and influential, and also a committed Zionist.

4. A man called Piet Brouwer works for him and Piet Brouwer visits London regularly.

And Johannesburg was a town he enjoyed.

He packed expertly over a final drink, then he went to his bed and slept eight hours. He slept poorly on aircraft and guessed he might need them.

Nevertheless he was sharply alert as he sat in the big man's visitors' chair. Russell had called as a matter of courtesy and also from a more private motive. For the moment the courtesy headed the list, since not to have made a formal call would have certainly raised the big man's eyebrows. There were people, not always exactly informed, who considered that what the big man ran was a wholly unscrupulous secret police, but Russell wasn't one of them and in any case he'd have made this call. You could tag them with what label you chose but indubitably they were very efficient, and it wouldn't have escaped their net that a man called Charles Russell had flown in without notice. No doubt he was retired by now and had come privately for a private wedding. Just the same he was Charles Russell still, not himself overkeen on a senseless formality but a stickler for the protocol which foreign colleagues might consider mattered. Not to have called would look almost suspicious and the last thing Charles Russell wished was suspicion. These people were very good indeed.

So he looked round the big rather featureless room and at the massive male behind the desk. Russell had never met him before since the man who had been his opposite number in his own tenure of the Security Executive had like Russell retired to a decent obscurity. The solid man said in excellent English though it was clear that it wasn't the language he dreamt in:

'It is really most kind to have called.'

'Not at all.'

'I trust that you had an agreeable flight.'

'As agreeable as any night flight can be.'

'And the drive from Johannesburg?'

'Perfect, thank you. Most considerate to have sent that car. The driver, by the way, was first class.'

The big man ignored the comment blandly and Charles Russell concealed a secret smile. The driver had been an African so his competence or lack of it was a matter of less than prime importance. Charles Russell like any man born of woman made mistakes though seldom the same one twice, and the smile was not at the big man's expense but at a boob which he'd once contrived himself. It had been his first time in South Africa and again they'd sent a car for him, so Russell, determined to play it safe, had climbed in at the back feeling faintly foolish, leaving the African driver to drive him. The African had looked mildly surprised but his manners had been excellent and it was Russell who had sweated first. For as they drove through the grander suburbs to town Charles Russell could see he'd decided wrongly. The local gentry and nobility were passing them in a lordly way, in enormous cars and all with black drivers, and *baas* was mostly in front with the African, chatting him up apparently happily. But in the office itself there'd been two damned great lifts, one marked *Whites* and the second the awful other thing. Charles Russell hadn't thought this wicked, he wasn't a man fond of moral judgements; he'd simply thought it obsessively wasteful.

So this time he'd gone in front with the African, feeding him cigarettes and small talk. Had that been reported? Probably yes. That sort of thing might be somehow significant.

The big man was saying with slow solemnity: 'As I understand it you are here quite privately.'

'There's no other way I could be here. I've come for a wedding—Mrs Meyer's daughter.'

'Ah.' There'd been the first flicker of genuine interest and more. 'You know Lester Meyer?'

'I haven't yet met him but I know Mrs Meyer. I knew her quite well once before her first marriage.'

'I see,' the big man said and waited.

Charles Russell began to feel his way since he hadn't called only for reasons of protocol. This man could give him information—he could, that is, if he thought it proper. Russell's guess was that he probably wouldn't; he had no illusions on where he stood. South Africans when they came to England insisted that the old tensions had gone, the mistrust between the two white races. What mattered today, or they'd have you think so, was the distinction of politics, Right or Left. Were you what they absurdly called a liberal or were you still trapped in the ancient *laagers*? That was the only division which counted, the rest was dead wood and had fallen away. That was what they always said. Sometimes they even seemed to believe it.

Russell knew you were very unwise to accept it. As a man whose native tongue was English he'd been suspect before he'd opened the door, perhaps not today as a matter of principle but the instinctive mistrust was deep-rooted as ever. He spoke English with an English accent, but that in its odd way was also a help. If he'd spoken through a local nose this man would have wished him good day by now. Russell said in his most English English:

'No, I've never met Meyer, I very much want to. He sounds a really remarkable man.'

'He's that, all right.'

There was a moment of silence and Russell waited, conscious that the balance was trembling. This man could rise smiling and hold out his hand, and Russell hadn't another card in his own. Or there was just the chance that he'd dare to unbend. Even to go on talking was something.

The moment of decision passed slowly, then the big man's powerful voice went on. 'You're Colonel Charles Russell and very experienced. You're experienced in another world. When you've met Lester Meyer I'd be pleased if you'd lunch with me.' He held up a hand as Russell stiffened. 'Not information—I couldn't ask that.'

'Then what would you want?'

'Your impression of Meyer.'

'I'll give it if you'll give me yours.'

For the first time the big man's smile was warm. 'Perfectly fair,' he said; he considered. 'I'm an Afrikaner as no doubt you'll have noticed.' His English was rather less formal now, not colloquial but not actively stilted. 'I'm of *voortrekker* stock and I don't much love *uitlanders*. Nor for that matter did President Kruger, whose home you should visit to understand us. And Meyer is the classic *uitlander*, the foreigner who breaks in, unwelcome.'

'I've been to President Kruger's house. It told me what books would not have done.'

'So?' There was another and visible relaxation. 'Then Meyer arrives in a threadbare shirt and in a very few years he's amassed a fortune. He's one of our richest men by now, but he's no more a part of my world than you are.'

'Stern words.'

'I know.' He smiled again. 'In Afrikaans they sound less unconvincing.'

Charles Russell had started to like this man. At first he had tended to write him down, just the senior but not quite secure official taking refuge behind a too formal manner. He had seen it before and been unimpressed. But now he'd begun to see a person, stolid and probably over-careful, but not without a cool dry humour. And Russell could understand his ethos. . . . The rest of the world is wrong, we are right. Russell didn't agree, he thought it absurd, but the view had a sort of exploded grandeur, startlingly uncontemporary but not for that reason alone mistaken. God put us here and that ends all argument.

As no doubt it did if you granted the premise.

Charles Russell began on a delicate probe. 'You said that you wouldn't ask information.'

'Why should I about a man like Meyer? He's enormously wealthy, successful, established.'

'But assimilated?'

For an instant the big man checked, then laughed. 'That's a very shrewd question—you frighten me. If you'd asked me as you came through that door I wouldn't have dreamt of answering, but as I've asked for your own impression of Meyer I'll answer you with another question. Is any good Jew ever quite assimilated? And you mustn't think I'm an anti-Semite. This society would fall apart at the seams if there were anything even approaching a pogrom.'

Russell knew this was entirely true. If the balance of economic power, the almost autonomous mining houses, were quietly being changed and tamed, the professions were bespoken still, the doctors, the lawyers, even the orchestra. There were people who wouldn't regret the last, but Johannesburg couldn't survive for a week without hospitals, courts, accountants and lawyers.

Charles Russell stood up and began to move, a technique which he'd learnt from a Russian colleague. He intended to ask his first direct question, and standing and on the point of leaving there'd be less loss of face if the big man declined it.

'Will you tell me how Meyer made his money?'

But the big man didn't immediately duck it. 'How *do* men like that make several millions? You can't mention a South African industry without mentioning one of Meyer's interests. But he started in diamonds as most of them do. I can tell you that since it's common knowledge.'

'And diamonds,' Charles Russell said, 'are portable.'

This time the senior official froze. 'In South Africa it is quite illegal to hold an uncut stone without a licence.'

'I knew that already.'

'Then why the question? I have to assume it was a question.'

'I was curious,' Charles Russell said.

'Curiosity can be very dangerous.'

'In another man's manor it is also impertinent. It would be, that is, if pursued improperly.'

'Is that an assurance?'

'Yes, it is.'

The big man unfroze at once; he smiled. 'Portable, yes— I agree to that. Exportable would be *very* different. So if there's anything we can ever do . . .'

'There's the very small matter of Maurice Pater.'

'You think that's a very small matter? Good. Since you're what you are I needn't conceal from you. I've heard rumours about Maurice Pater which would disturb me very much indeed if I happened to feel they were my concern. As it is I'm inclined to think they are not. Any troubles of Mr Maurice Pater are no more a concern of mine than would diamonds, if you'll let me say so, be a proper concern of Colonel Russell.'

'You don't think his troubles might follow him here?'

'I think it very unlikely indeed. But if they were to you wouldn't find us helpless.'

Charles Russell went back to the car and Johannesburg. . . . So the big man would keep a cool eye on Pater, not so much because he feared any danger as because of the system he stoutly defended. For Pater was British, a Member, a journalist, and the local word for Maurice Pater was liberal and a very rude one. The big man wouldn't want Pater troublesome so he'd watch where he went and he'd watch his contacts, and given the big man's local politics Charles

Russell thought this wholly reasonable. Moreover it killed two birds with one stone. A watched Maurice Pater would be also a safe one. Excellent. Russell had come from a sense of duty. Now he'd enjoy an agreeable holiday.

12

The man whom his agents called the *patron* had slipped back into Paris and sent for Georges Bresse. He kissed him ritually on both cheeks, then said:

'I apologize.'

'For not being here? That was perfectly natural.'

'No, something more personal—I shouldn't have sent you. To London, I mean, but we needed the money.'

'I've another eight hundred here for you.'

'Keep it. They've paid us.'

Bresse looked at the *patron*, his spirits rising. Only this man and his own conviction kept him working for an organization which he knew very well was at best third rate, but he had given his deepest loyalty freely since there wasn't another altar to serve at, and he had given it unequivocally though aware of the *patron*'s more obvious failings—his suspiciousness, an unbending logic and the conviction he shared with Said Abdul Jawal that every man's hand was of course against him. But that was all that he shared with Said Abdul Jawal. The *patron* was a Bedouin, and though he spoke French and wore English suits no man could have thought he was anything else. This whiff of the desert he mostly played down, since nothing worse served the Arab cause than a belief that they were romantic nomads, the heroes of mildly erotic fiction. But he couldn't escape a most striking appearance, the great height, the lean face and the hard dark eye. Said Abdul Jawal in the robes of his race had looked what he was, an unpleasant clerk, but the *patron* in European clothes had no need of these props to hold Georges Bresse. The *patron* had something more potent and used it, a magic which could command men's hearts.

It had occurred to Georges Bresse who by blood was half Frenchman that one day there would be other leaders, more worldly, more expert and even more ruthless. There would but they wouldn't inspire his love.

Even if he were alive to see them.

But the *patron* was repeating himself. 'Yes, we needed the money and needed it badly. But if I'd known what a muddle they'd make I'd never have loaned you or anyone else.'

'I'm sorry it turned out such a shambles.'

'Not your fault—it was totally misconceived. To try to win Pater's support was sound but to offer him money directly was childish. It should have been possible to engage his interest—after all we've a very good case indeed—and then there'd be half a dozen ways to bind him to our side securely.' The *patron* shrugged. 'Set up some Institution or other, some Society with a magniloquent title. Make him President or maybe Secretary—a small salary and perhaps a car. Not that either of those would have bound Maurice Pater, he'd have given them up if he thought he ought to. But he'd never accept a loss of face, an admission that he'd decided wrongly. Once identified we'd have him for ever. And to try to use violence was simply madness.'

'The violence got out of hand.'

'I know.'

Said Abdul Jawal had not been mentioned. The *patron* knew, he could hardly fail to, but he'd ignored the matter as unimportant. He'd shared Georges Bresse's dislike of the man and he actively hated his distant master. Who had money which he would sometimes dole out but played the ends against the middle cravenly. An anachronism, a man to forget: *ergo* one forgot his servant. The *patron* had known Georges Bresse had been wounded and he'd inquired for the wound with real concern, but how Georges Bresse had come by it had been something he hadn't wished to discuss. He had known of course, and a man was dead. But the man had been an irrelevance. Leave it.

'How much does my failure matter?' Bresse asked.

'I don't think you failed in any way, you were set an entirely impossible mission. Nevertheless the result is serious. What's been done is to turn a potential friend into an open and influential enemy, and look at it how you will that's bad. And Maurice Pater's power to damage isn't limited to our public relations.'

'What else could he do?'

'A great deal. I'll tell you.'

He began to do so with something like passion; he began to talk, as Russell had written, of the real sinews of the State of Israel. In fact it lived and fought wars on subsidies and these subsidies came from several sources. Each had a character quite unique, one sent in a conscious and furious loyalty, another as a reluctant sop to a conscience the donor believed he'd forgotten. . . . You'd made a very good life in a land you'd been born in, then why should you fight for your blood in a strange one? So you sent it some money and hoped to sleep tightly, and perhaps when you didn't you sent some more.

All this was common knowledge, accepted: it was the mechanics which were much more interesting. For these sums were very large indeed and not every State welcomed the steady drain. In America it was still straightforward, you could even claim some relief of tax if you put your gift down to an authorized charity. But there were countries where this wasn't so, where the authorities would be forced to take action if they were faced with real knowledge of what went on. And the important words were 'forced' and 'knowledge'. A politician or a wise official could suspect and decide to hold his hand but if you nailed it to his desk he'd be forced to act. So naturally you didn't do so.

South Africa, for instance. Consider. Johannesburg was a great Jewish city, comparable, if not in numbers, to the city of New York itself, and there was a highly respectable organization, accepted officially, perfectly scrupulous, which collected donations and sent them away. It sent them across the exchanges openly.

And could Bresse or indeed any man of their cause accept that this was the final tally? To do so would be very ingenuous when that war would have stretched a State richer than Israel.

'Then how does the rest come out?' Bresse asked.

'I suspect Lester Meyer smuggles out diamonds. Naturally there's no proof or we'd use it. The South Africans wouldn't stand for that, not even from a Lester Meyer. But it's a matter of simple logic.'

'Then this must be stopped. Lester Meyer——'

'No.' The *patron* shook his distinguished head. 'Cut that thorn down and another springs up. Moreover, if Meyer died by violence the connection would be much too clear. *We* have a motive, *we* should be suspect.' The *patron* held a hand up, smiling. 'No, the key to this is Meyer's carriers. The death of just one would stop it all if that death were dramatic enough to be frightening. Meyer wouldn't then find another easily.'

'That's logical,' Bresse said.

It was. An Englishman, if one had been present, would have listened impressed but also sceptical. The reasoning was as hard as a diamond but diamonds weren't Englishmen's favourite stones. Besides, they'd been talking in French. That was suspect. It was a lapidary language but an Englishman would mistrust it instinctively. And Gallic logic in the mouths of Arabs . . .

Georges Bresse had been thinking and now he spoke. 'So you'd like me to take out Brouwer?'

'That's a little too late to have much point. Brouwer's marrying into the Meyer family, and though Meyer's a long way from caricature he's still a very Jewish Jew. There are plenty of ways he can still employ Brouwer but he won't use him again for running diamonds.'

'Then whom will he use?'

'He'll use Maurice Pater.'

The Englishman who wasn't present would have raised a hand to hide a smile but Bresse was half a Frenchman still and if the *patron* thought that then he must have a reason. All Bresse did was to raise a mild objection.

'A British Member of Parliament?'

'Quite. What Customs man would venture to search him? And as for his motive, you've read his speeches, you'll have seen those really damaging articles. He's gone over to our enemy wholly. And if that isn't enough remember that interview, the one he gave on television.' The *patron* began to quote in English. '*You mustn't misunderstand me, though. I'll do anything I can to help.*'

'Yes, I heard him say that.'

'Is it not enough?'

'But how do we know for certain?'

'We don't just yet—only time will tell us. Pater went out for his daughter's wedding but it's what happens after the wedding that matters. If he postpones his return for any reason. . . . He isn't at all the type of man to stay on in that country because he liked it.'

'How shall we know if he stays?'

'We shall. I've got nobody in South Africa whom I'd trust with anything really serious but I've somebody who can check Pater's movements. In point of fact it's a local woman.'

'A woman?' Bresse said. In his trade he mistrusted them.

'I know what you're thinking but think again.'

Lester Meyer had a dressing-room and having used it he opened the bedroom door. He'd expected to find his wife asleep but she was propped up on pillows, not even reading.

'Thinking about the wedding?' he asked.

'No, the wedding's all organized. Not the wedding.'

She was staring at the ceiling intently. There were painted *amorini* there in poses which Lester thought improbable, staring in their turn at the room which clearly they didn't entirely credit. There were certainly people who wouldn't have liked it. The censorious would have muttered crossly, some cliché about conspicuous waste, and persons of delicate taste would have started. All the Louis were there and some Empire too, but the dressing-table was starkly modern and the enormous bed had come straight from London. Neither Lester nor Miriam cared a curse. The room was superbly comfortable and it suited their respective auras.

'What's on your mind?'

'Maurice Pater is.'

'I can't think why, he's quite safe out here.'

'That's the point. I'd like to keep him here.'

He could see she had more than the seeds of a plan. 'But would he accept that?'

'I know how to make him.'

'You'd do that to him?'

'I would for his good.'

'Considering you're three-quarters Gentile the other quarter's remarkably potent.'

'If it hadn't been you wouldn't have married me.'

'That's perfectly true.' He climbed into bed. 'I should sleep on it,' he said.

'I mean to.'

He turned out the light and composed himself comfortably; he knew better than to press her now; he said with affectionate resignation: 'Let me know when you've got it all worked out.'

'Of course I will, I shall need your help.'

13

Maurice Pater had been very careful. In the world which he moved in he wasn't thought Left, but he realized that in South Africa there'd be people who took the ingenuous view that if you didn't whole-heartedly back their system you were probably a secret communist. And he had personal motives to tread very warily. For one thing he was old-fashioned enough to believe that a guest had obligations. This was formally a friendly country and he could enter it freely without a visa. It would be very bad manners to knock it openly. And for another his daughter was marrying here, she had a life to make and he hoped she'd be happy. It was out of the question to prejudice that.

Nevertheless he disliked South Africa, though not for the reasons he'd cherished in London. Expatriate South Africans and the protagonists of the new African States were often both vocal and tiresomely pressing, but it was clear that if you swallowed their views your judgement could be well off centre. The sensible thing was to do a Three Monkeys—hear nothing, see nothing, guard your tongue. No doubt that was something well short of heroic, but if you had a daughter here, if your private position inhibited action, it was better than endless futile talk. Besides, the longer you stayed the more you doubted. To see this extraordinary country too simply, as a question of Black versus White, was a trap. There was also the Indian problem—insoluble. It was curious, Maurice Pater reflected, that wherever the Indian went he was loathed. Guyana and now East Africa, Malaya and Singapore, Hong Kong. They kept shops and lent money, entangling customers. They were clannish and their women chaste. Much worse than that they worked too hard.

Just the same Maurice Pater had made his judgement, though not for the reasons he'd heard in Earls Court. It was easy to say that this very strange people were out of the stream and therefore suspect, but they were out of the stream in another sense too. There'd been kings who had fought for their absolute power, aristocracies which had clung to privilege. All were gone, all were dead, they were part of history. But there hadn't before been a peasant oligarchy. Harsh verdict? He believed it true.

And really they were absurdly wasteful. Maurice Pater had been up to the high veldt and it had shaken him more than the African townships. He had gone to visit a great-uncle's grave, an old man he had liked and could just remember. He'd been a trooper in a regiment of Lancers and contemptuous of his well-born commanders. . . . The Boers wouldn't stand a cavalry charge? Of course they bloody wouldn't, why should they? So the magnificent Lancers went galloping through and got shot to shreds in the simplest ambush. And most of the time they weren't Lancers anyway. The veldt had been hot and the horses too big. Most of the time the men had marched but carrying their horses' saddles. Pater's great-uncle told it with casual malice, but after the war he'd gone back and married. He'd married an Afrikaner girl and his brothers had said that the man had gone native.

He had seen his great-uncle's crumbling grave but to get there he'd had to cross much country and it had horrified him as Johannesburg hadn't. Johannesburg was a big brash city and people who disapproved of it would disapprove of most American towns, but Pater had come from farming stock and though he'd never himself worked land directly the high veldt had hit him hard where it hurt. Just hundreds of miles of almost nothing, cattle but not the high-yielding strains, flocks of sheep when you saw them and patches of mealie. It was the classic extensive, near-nomad farming and the names on the gates were Afrikaner. Pater liked to be well-informed when he could and he'd listened to all the explanations. Much of the grass was the sour-grass and tricky; it wouldn't safely feed cattle the whole year round. Other grass had been tried but it hadn't succeeded, and if you tried to lea in the English manner you lost your topsoil in the first high wind. Above all there was the lack of water. There were long dry months which saw no rain, and although there were artesian wells very few gave more than a marginal yield and fewer still were a source you could really rely on.

All this was quite true and quite unanswerable. Maurice Pater had accepted it, for he'd seen figures and graphs, very willingly shown him. His mind was convinced but his viscera doubted. Put Israelis on this difficult tract and somehow they'd make it flourish mightily. Or almost any Oriental. Somehow they'd get the water there, carrying it in petrol cans, from God knew where but they'd find it and bring it. He remembered what he'd said in the House, that land best belonged to the man who best used it. If that were true, and he really believed it, then the title of these upland barons was alarmingly short of indefeasible.

But he'd been too circumspect to express his thoughts, which made him angrier than he would have been when he realized he was being followed. He'd been dining alone, quite pleased to do so; he didn't find Miriam's world offensive but he did find it strange and at times rather frightening. It was simply that it had different values. So he'd been eating in an Italian restaurant and afterwards gone to a sell-out revue for which Miriam had somehow procured a ticket. And the show had quite astounded Pater. In London they'd tirelessly rubbed it in—South Africa was a gross Police State. Well, perhaps it was but a very odd one. In Hitler's Reich this crisp revue would never have been allowed to open, and if you preferred not to think of Hitler's Reich then in Spain today they'd have shut it down. In Italy there'd have been a riot. For the Prime Minister had been guyed without mercy, bitterly and even scandalously, and the audience had laughed their heads off, quite freely, not looking across their shoulders once. It was true that in the bar in the interval Pater had heard only English spoken, but the fact remained that the show went on and it was very hard indeed to get tickets. Yet in England he'd heard a South African clergyman explaining to such as cared to listen that the reason his Rugby football team had failed to defeat the degenerate English was that the Almighty had glimpsed a mini-skirt and had naturally shown divine displeasure.

He had left the theatre, deciding to walk, since the night was fine and he needed some air. And just before the top of Claim Street he noticed the girl who was plodding behind him.

His first feeling was one of extreme injustice. He'd been a paragon of careful discretion yet the police had been tailing him after all; and then came the humiliation—he'd judged it wrong, they'd been right in London. This was a real Police State after all.

He swung on his heel and the woman saw him. She slipped left into Van der Merwe Street. Pater wasn't much scared but quietly furious. He walked on for maybe twenty yards, then turned again and stood his ground. The woman behind was again on station.

Pater looked at her as she closed the distance and his certainty dissolved in doubt. She hadn't the air of the police at all and this was Hillbrow and he'd heard talk of it— determined to be somehow with it, to a Londoner's eye rather charmingly innocent but to the burghers of this splendid city not a matter they wished to discuss with a stranger.

He could see the girl's face as she came on quietly. She was really rather a pretty one. In the highly selective local sense she was certainly what was called a White but Pater didn't believe she was European. She had very dark hair and a dense sallow skin. And he was certain now that she wasn't police. She was a woman of a much older profession.

His anger melted in a gentle relief, this was something he could easily handle. He stood perfectly still and the girl saw him waiting. She hesitated: he saw her decide. She put a hand in her pocket and came on steadily.

Lester Meyer was going to bed again. He was short of sleep as he often was but he saw that his wife was determined to talk. 'I've been thinking,' she said.

'Then you'd better tell me.'

'If Maurice goes back to England they'll get him.'

'Aren't you pitching that a little high? These things blow over, the heat subsides.'

'With any ordinary man that's perfectly true but I know Maurice Pater much better than you do. Convince him that there's a moral issue and he'll ride it right into the ground, himself with it. And you know how the other side thinks.'

'I do.' He considered it for some time in silence. 'It would be easy to say you're chasing a ghost but there are people who believe in ghosts. Idealists like Maurice are dangerous and we're talking of very revengeful people.'

'Whereas here he'd be perfectly safe?'

'Very probably. The sort of man who would want to harm him is the sort who could hardly get into this country. His own doesn't have a consulate here and I doubt if he'd even be given a visa. He might slip across a frontier but the Special Branch are as sharp as razors.'

'It scares me to hear you say it,' she said.

He knew what she meant, he'd been running some risk. It wasn't that he'd been breaking the law, or not more than most wealthy men constantly broke it. Rich men thought of wealth as a simple commodity, something which passed across frontiers freely, and if States indulged strange economic theories which made that free passage difficult, then States were asking the impossible and there was no great sin in defeating stupidity. If diamonds had been the only way then Meyer would have smuggled diamonds. The *patron* had been perfectly right, not in fact as it happened but reading Meyer.

She had guessed but had never mentioned it, caring no more than her splendid husband for the niceties of exchange control. 'Is that over now?' she asked him softly.

'I know what you mean.' He never ducked. 'Yes, it's over now, the need has passed.'

'Let's drink to that.'

'A fine idea.'

He left the room laughing, returning with open bottle and glasses. He knew perhaps six words of Hebrew and two of them he used to her now.

She answered him as she drank the wine. 'Tonight I shall sleep for a change,' she said.

'Sleep well but let's finish the other thing first.'

'Oh, Maurice.' But she hadn't forgotten. 'Could you find him a job here?'

'I could if you asked me.'

'Down in the Cape? He'd be happier there.'

He smiled as he poured more wine for them both. So she thought that the Cape would be Pater's country. 'There's a peninsula there which juts out in the sea and houses with people with lots of *angst*. Much wringing of hands but they don't do a thing. They like the life too well to risk it. In any case I don't have connections there.'

'Then the law, perhaps?'

'Not really on. He could qualify, I imagine, and try, but he'd hardly learn Afrikaans at his age and it's a competitive bar which Maurice isn't.'

'Then what would you do?'

'Would you leave it to me? I'd speak to Tom who would talk to Dick, and if that didn't work Dick would speak to Harry.'

'Enough to live on?'

'Enough to start. After that it would be up to him.'

'So he'd need a bit of capital? For a house—all that?'

'You were thinking of making a present?'

'No. I was thinking of how to make him agree.'

'We skirmished around his agreement before.' Meyer knew the whole story, she'd told him everything. Neither Russell nor Tuke had asked her not to. She wasn't the type which gossiped foolishly but equally she would tell a husband, especially when he was Lester Meyer.

'I know we did and you told me to tell you. You told me to say when I'd worked it out.'

She started to talk and he listened, astonished. His wife could still astonish him and it was something he privately relished still.

'You remember they shot him a bribe? In cash. Twenty thousand pounds of it.'

'I remember that—it started the story.'

'Then what do you think he did with the money?'

He hadn't thought of that and frankly said so. He'd been busy and stretched on the rack of risk and Maurice Pater had come from another world. He'd been too troubled to think of Maurice Pater's.

'I can only think what I wouldn't do. I couldn't put it in a bank with safety and if I kept it I'd be at risk for ever.'

'Would you give it to your solicitor?'

'I could ask you if any lawyer would take it.'

'Not as a lawyer, perhaps. As a friend. As a man who admired your peculiar virtues but felt that in a wicked world you needed any help you could get.'

'But no lawyer would hold it for ever—uncovered. There'd have to be a time limit.'

'Quite.'

'My God,' he said, 'you *have* thought it out.'

They began to discuss it with easy freedom, as a practical

business proposition. Over any big deal he had always consulted her, not because he believed she would grasp all the details but because he believed she had natural judgement. So they discussed Pater now as a proposition, a property in which Miriam Meyer was thinking of taking an active interest. She would be, that is, if the interest was on, and that meant on by business standards.

'His lawyer's the same as mine,' she said. 'I sent him there and he gave him some briefs.'

'And you needn't remind me he's now mine too.'

'What's the London end of your business worth to him?'

'Rather more than he'd care to lose, I think. But he's much too established to squeeze directly.'

'I wasn't suggesting you squeeze him directly. That's there in the background and therefore useful, but if we're right about a time limit then our solicitor has a very good reason to get rid of the money before it bites him.'

'I can't ring him up, bang, and suggest that he send it here.'

'Of course you can't—that's much too crude. But it wouldn't be crude just to let him know, I mean that we've guessed he's got Maurice's bribe. The mere fact that another person suspects would start any sane solicitor worrying.' She looked at him with a good wife's affection. 'You'll know exactly how to put it over.'

He laughed again. 'Perhaps I do. But I don't think it follows our lawyer will panic.'

'I don't ask that the wretched man should panic, or not on the first approach to him. I want him to send a cable to Maurice, remind him that there *is* a time limit.'

'And then?'

'Then I'll have a little talk with Maurice. If necessary I'll tell him everything, the bits of the story he doesn't know— trying to put him into hospital and then the attempt to kidnap Barbara. Morally he's very brave but in physical matters he's not a hero. And with a suitable job all set for him here . . .'

'You think he'd give up his career?'

'What career?'

Meyer said for the second time: 'You'd do that to him?'

'I would for his good. I would indeed.'

'And the solicitor?'

'We'll increase the pressures.'

'Such as what?'

'Such as race, for instance. Friends in common.'

He poured the last of the wine and again raised his glass. 'I wouldn't fancy you as an enemy.'

'Thank you.'

The girl had hated it and had tried to duck but her sister had nagged till she'd given in. By blood she was a Lebanese but she'd never seen her father's country nor nourished the least desire to do so. She was part of a small but accepted community and she asked no more of the life she knew than what she'd been born to take from it, a husband, a home and a houseful of children. She had a job as a stenographer; she was modest and unassuming, Christian. The language of the home was English, or sometimes her father would still speak French. She didn't know a word of Arabic or trouble her head about Arab politics. All that was in another world.

Till her sister had met that dreadful man. He'd been a steward on a cruising ship and one of her ports of call had been Durban. Moreover he'd been a distant cousin, and when he'd come up on shore-leave to visit them her father had at first been delighted. She knew that he wasn't delighted now, for this man had turned her sister's head. Not with love, though there might be a hint of that, but with ideas which she'd promptly swallowed blindly. He'd been bursting with talk of the Arab cause, how the rulers of Arab States were useless, how salvation lay only in people's wars. She had thought it a froth of dangerous bombast but this man had hooked her sister helplessly. Who now talked like he did and sometimes more wildly. They were Arabs, weren't they? They had their duty.

The girl didn't think she was Arab at all but her sister was the stronger character. She worked as a telephonist in the hotel where a man called Pater was staying, and this Pater was an enemy, a friend of the Jews, their running dog. She had learnt the jargon alarmingly pat. So this Pater had come out to South Africa, ostensibly for his daughter's wedding, but of course he couldn't be trusted an inch, in South Africa or anywhere else. He'd done enough damage in England already, so it was necessary to watch him here. The task she'd been given was very simple: she listened to his telephone calls and she'd pass on any news of importance. She'd be ashamed to do anything less for her people.

So far there had been nothing to pass, but tonight he'd booked a table at Mario's and it was known that politicians ate there. She was on duty herself and she couldn't get off, but the bug of the amateur agent had bitten her. This was the pay-off, the crisis—it must be. Mario's—a whole gang of them went there. They probably wouldn't talk freely in public, but it was where Maurice Pater went afterwards. . . . Vital. Vital to the Arab cause, to the inalienable rights of a deathless people.

The girl had considered this foolish nonsense but her sister had nattered on and on and she was capable of making scenes. The girl's mother was dead, her father ailing, and she shrank from a domestic upheaval. Finally they had struck a compromise. Very well, she would follow Maurice Pater, from Mario's to his hotel—no more. If he called on the way she would note the address. Beyond that she wouldn't budge and didn't.

So now she was walking up Claim Street glumly, aware

that the man in front had noticed her. He was standing quite still and silently waiting. She hadn't the least idea what to do. Turn tail and run? He might call the police. Somehow they might contrive to trace her and she'd been educated to fear the police. There was nothing to do but walk on and hope.

Maurice Pater stood rigid and watched her come nearer. He had thought she was something to do with the police, then he'd thought she was simply a prowling tart. Now he wasn't so certain, she hadn't the air. In the light from the street lamps he saw her face clearly. She was pretty but she wasn't painted. If this was a tart . . .

What else could she be? No police force would use such an untrained tail. The relief he had felt was now sour resentment for he'd remembered the woman who'd burst into his flat, the terrible breath, that scandalous photograph. This was another. She must be. She was.

As she came level he said it brutally:

'Some other time. I'm tired tonight.'

The girl stared at him in utter shame. Her face began to fall to pieces. Finally she started to run. She swung on her heel and she ran in horror.

14

In the matter of Mr Maurice Pater the big man had said that he wouldn't be helpless, so Russell had settled quietly down to what he thought of now as a welcome holiday. His views on the South African scene weren't such as to spoil the pleasure he took in it, unless of course he made moral judgements, which to Russell were the last anathema. It was a pity that sometimes defensible ends were pursued with what struck him as clumsy zeal, and the overtones of a strange religion, the conviction the Lord of Hosts stood behind you, were something which made him conceal a shudder. But neither were matters to spoil a vacation. It wasn't a country he wished to live in but nor was it one which he burned to condemn. In private he was often critical, but no man had set him up in judgement and he wasn't by nature a doctrinaire.

So Russell had been enjoying himself, but keeping the tempo apt for his age. He'd declined most of the social invitations which through Miriam had come showering down, but he'd been to the races, he'd played some golf, and it was agreeable just to sit in the sun in the pleasantest hotel garden he knew. He wasn't a very keen racing man but had greatly enjoyed what the Turf Club had offered, the blue-painted roofs in the clear strong sun, the crowd which was openly having fun, not the lugubrious pros of an English racecourse. And the Turf Club had an air all its own, a flavour between a northern point-to-point and a straight-forward meeting on Ascot Heath unconcerned with the fact that a month ago the place had been rather tiresomely Royal. On top of that one could watch the horses. They didn't appear to have specialists here, a horse was a horse as God had made him, and if he happened to be a good one, fine. One Saturday he'd be sprinting five furlongs and on the next in a race of a mile and a quarter. And they ran them up very fine indeed.

The golf had been interesting too in its way. Russell had been often warned that these greens had a heavy nap on them, but in fact he had found it less than expected. What had worried him had been hitting an iron shot. He liked to pinch the ball and here he couldn't, the grass was too thick, there was nothing to hit against. You had to sweep them away and Charles Russell couldn't, the knack of it just wouldn't come. He hadn't played quite so badly for years, but he was playing for pleasure not earning his living.

He was sitting in the garden this morning planning the last few days of his stay. He looked at his diary; he had just a week left. The wedding was tomorrow, Thursday, and nothing would have kept him away from it. It would be large and maybe a trifle brash, which meant it would be a splendid wedding, the sort of big jolly Charles Russell enjoyed. After that he'd slip down to the Mooi River, to a hotel he liked and country he knew, and he'd hire a car and drive up to the Drakensberg . . .

An African was standing before him, uniformed and saluting smartly. He gave Charles Russell a long sealed envelope.

It was a message from the big man again and Russell hadn't expected to hear from him. He'd been asked for his impression of Meyer but he hadn't believed he'd be pressed to give it; the request had been an experienced gambit, something to start the conversation on lines which the big man had wished to follow. And also he'd spoken of lunching together but Charles Russell hadn't taken it seriously. Yet this message was politely urgent.

The African waited till Russell had read it; he saluted again. 'I have a car, sir.'

'I'll come at once. Please wait while I change.'

Now Russell was in the impersonal office. The big man said:

'You were kind to come.'

'Not at all. I had nothing else to do.' This wasn't quite true, he had cancelled a lunch date, but he despised any byplay of hard to get.

'First I owe you my thanks.'

'Whatever for?'

'You gave me an assurance—you've kept it. You remember we talked of a certain matter? I believe that I made myself fairly clear.'

'You were perfectly clear though you weren't explicit.'

The big man poured strong and excellent coffee. 'In our trade it seldom pays to be that, though I do recollect that we used the word diamonds. Your disinterest in diamonds, Colonel, has been remarkable and indeed exemplary.'

'How do you know?'

The big man looked mildly surprised but shrugged. 'You can't really believe that a man like yourself could arrive in this country without causing, well, interest.'

Charles Russell was in no way resentful. He was thinking of a friend of his, like himself well disposed to this country but critical, who'd discovered what he'd called a Law. The Law ran like this and he'd sworn it was true: plain-clothes members of the Special Branch will sit in the fourth row but not behind it.

But Russell hadn't noticed one. The big man's people were certainly competent.

He asked amiably: 'So you've been checking me?'

'We've been checking your contacts—they've all been normal. You gave me your word that they would be so, so one of the reasons I've asked you here is to pay you back what I take as a kindness. It would really have been extremely awkward if Charles Russell had started to poke about.' The big man finished his coffee thoughtfully. 'The matter which we discussed is finished. It was spread across some weeks of crisis, and in any case it wasn't diamonds. Now I hold an undertaking from a source I am perfectly sure I can trust.'

'I'm delighted to hear it.'

'I thought you might be.'

Charles Russell let this pass in silence. The implication was that he'd come to South Africa with a formal interest in Meyer's affairs, whereas he'd come because of Maurice Pater, in effect to reassure himself that a decision he'd made wouldn't cost too dear. Pieter Brouwer and Lester Meyer himself had been pieces in the grand design, he'd suspected they fitted and now he knew it, but to Russell they were not the essentials. As for Meyer and this wise official it seemed probable he'd known more than he'd told, but if so the golden rule was his guide. As it had been to Charles Russell himself when he'd decided he'd have to let Bresse go. If forced to accept a scandal you did so but only on a balance of evils. And the cost of political scandals was high, especially when more than one country was caught in them, not a matter to leave to a Public Prosecutor. This big man had certainly thought so too.

He was agreeably relaxed by now, not feeling his way as he had been at first but treating Russell as an established colleague. 'But I've other news you may find less acceptable.'

'What's that?'

'It's Pater.'

'You suggested you'd keep an eye on him.'

'Yes and no.' The big man sent for fresh coffee and poured it. 'As I hinted before there are really two aspects. My own was that Pater shouldn't be foolish, and on that side I can reassure you. He hasn't put a foot wrong once. He's given interviews to a couple of papers but said nothing within a mile of regrettable, and they gave him a spot on the radio where he talked about the beautiful landscape, the climate, the hospitable people.'

'I thought he'd be sensible.'

'Yes, he has been. It's the other side that worries me, though.'

'We had hoped that there wouldn't be one here.'

'Not to exaggerate—simply to tell you. I told you before I'd heard stories about him, rumours which would have troubled me if his safety in England were my affair. But I thought he'd be perfectly safe in South Africa, if only because his enemies aren't a race which can enter the country freely. Most of the time he's been moving in company and it was never a question of actively guarding him. But we're a cautious folk as I dare say you've noticed and one night we heard he was dining alone. That was something which called for a modest insurance, so I told a good man to keep an eye open.'

'There was trouble? You killed it?' Charles Russell had leant forward sharply.

'Not trouble, just something you ought to know. This man of mine kept an eye on Pater and he noticed that somebody else was too.'

'Rather a striking man? French accent?'

'You are interested in such a one? No, it wasn't a man at all but a girl. In point of fact a Lebanese.'

Russell said crisply: 'Record?'

'None. Two sisters who live with a widowed father. Nothing against them of any kind.'

'But Lebanese . . .'

'I follow your thought. So I'll tell you what I propose to do. There could easily be nothing in this, but I *have* heard rumours and Pater's a Member. The last thing we want here is complications so for the first time I've put a real guard on him. That will last till he flies out on Friday evening. After that it's your problem not mine, thank God.'

'I'll see it's passed on where it matters in England.'

'I thought you should know it for what it's worth.'

'I'm really very grateful indeed.'

The big man rose. 'And now to luncheon. I don't expect you like our meat. Considering how much we eat it's astonishing we can't breed it better.'

Maurice Pater returned from the wedding depressed. It had been big and convivial, a social occasion, and Charles Russell had not been the only guest who had enjoyed it uninhibitedly. But Maurice Pater it had simply saddened. Conspicuous waste wasn't one of his clichés nor envy one of his private vices, but this tremendous jolly had rubbed it in, that he could never take root in this sunny world. Not that he had intended to but he had intended to visit Barbara. It would have been pleasant to slip away from England when the fog clamped down and the endless grey sky, for a fortnight or maybe even a month, to sit in the sun and to play with his grandchildren. That was something he had looked forward to, but he doubted now that he'd ever do it. Miriam had given Barbara a house, not a big one but to Pater luxurious, and it was implicit that Pieter Brouwer himself would shortly be earning a handsome living. None of this made a visit impossible but it emphasized the essential difference. These people were extroverts: Pater was not. Barbara was marrying in a different life. For a time, no doubt, she'd be pleased to see him, but then, after a year or two. . . . The letter at breakfast, the look at her husband. 'Father's thinking of coming out again.' The shrug and the generous, dutiful answer. 'Then say yes, of course, but not for too long.'

Maurice Pater sighed softly; he wouldn't risk that.

He was thinking of trying to eat some dinner when an African came in with the cable. Maurice Pater compulsively over-tipped him, then he opened and read it, at first unbelieving. He was very badly shaken indeed.

It was a telegram from his lawyer in London and the last

thing he'd expected in Africa. It was guarded in wording but scaringly clear. A certain matter was still outstanding and a limit had been agreed to settle it. The twenty-one days were not yet exhausted but time was running against them strongly. Maurice Pater had given an undertaking and would realize his proper obligation. It was very polite and very formal but the warning was unmistakable. Dispose of that twenty thousand pounds or I'll be obliged to take action myself to do so.

That had been what they'd agreed between them, but Pater had almost forgotten it. Psychiatrists, he remembered now, had some theory that the things you forgot were no more than the things which you wished to suppress. That might well be true though quite unproven but in this case there'd been an acuter motive for sweeping the matter under the carpet. Quite simply he hadn't known what to do. When he got back to London he'd think; if he had to he'd go to Tuke again. Why worry about this embarrassing matter when in Africa he could do nothing about it?

As he sat on his bed he almost wept. He wasn't Maurice Pater now, fair-minded and moderate, liberal and decent; he was an atavism of this admirable figure, swamped by the impotent rage of clear conscience. They'd come at him and he hadn't invited it, and who were these bloody 'they' in any case? They talked of their wrongs, of inalienable rights, but in fact they were a historical backwater. It was an irony of the sardonic gods that beneath their appalling deserts lay oil. If they hadn't had that they'd have quietly destroyed themselves, by corruption, incompetence, pointless rivalries. Hundreds of thousands of acres of nothing, wretched soil when you could see it at all through a layer of all too human excrement. Then some deity on a wet afternoon needs a laugh and decides to give them oil. A great Power must have it and meant to do so, partly because of increasing need and partly because of brutal *realpolitik*, an economic defeat to the rivals it feared. So this people whom history had half forgotten is pushed back into the footlights, mouthing. Inalienable Arab lands, one whole and indivisible nation. Endlessly talking, endless bombast.

Pater checked himself; he was much ashamed. Subjective thinking was always unsound and at worst it could lead to unsound judgement. What he needed now was precise decision. In England there was Harry Tuke who owned known and very efficient resources. Perhaps they could somehow protect the innocent from a bribe which they'd unknowingly signed for. This was what he had hoped for but now he couldn't, now he'd have to do his thinking at once. It would have been one thing to go back for more help, quite another to be obliged to add that the pressure had come down already. Tuke wouldn't like that, no Minister would. It limited any assistance possible and it more than doubled the risks of giving it.

Maurice Pater wasn't happy in Africa but it was where he happened to find himself now and it was here he would have to do his thinking. He knew that to sit down at a desk, to try to force new ideas out of nothing, was fatal to any hope of invention. This wasn't like working a brief or White Paper. What he wanted was a fresh solution, not a careful assessment of facts known already. He'd slip away for a bit and let it come. Not Johannesburg, it stifled him mentally. It would have to be a total change.

On the night table there was a pile of brochures, for trips to this place and tours of that. He peeled off the topmost—the Kruger Park. Maurice Pater wasn't fond of wild life but if he wanted a change this would certainly be one.

He rang the airline to postpone his flight, then an agency to book his trip, and the girl on the hotel exchange, the sister of the other who'd tailed him, made a careful note and then went off duty. The man they called *patron* read her cable; he nodded and he sent for Georges Bresse.

Bresse went to him as he always did in a mood between exaltation and fear, the former for what the *patron* gave him, the instant lift in morale and faith, the fear because Georges Bresse knew well that this very strange man had a stranger power, an hypnotic gift to numb men's judgement. The *patron* gave him the cable and watched him read it. 'You see,' he said, 'how right we were. Pater has postponed his return and for that there can only be one explanation.'

Georges Bresse had been considering what the *patron* had said when they'd met before. It had appealed to both the men he was, the Frenchman who wanted to know the facts and the Arab with his driving compulsion to take action against the enemy—action. The established facts were to Bresse unassailable. It was a fact that vast sums had been poured into Israel, amounts which not every State could tolerate if presented to it openly as an item in the nation's accounts; it was a fact Lester Meyer was actively Zionist; it was a fact he was deep in the world of diamonds and employed a man called Pieter Brouwer whom he sent to and fro from London regularly though he hadn't the qualifications for business.

At this point the Frenchman surrendered, anaesthetized: the neurosis of action sank him tracelessly. From this point Georges Bresse wasn't asking questions; he was asking for opportunity, only grateful to this man who could offer it. But he still had a single doubt and put it.

'As a matter of logic, Meyer's the fountainhead. Wouldn't it be more decisive to go for Lester Meyer directly?'

'Perhaps it would but it wouldn't be practical.' In the *patron's* mouth the word had an irony, but Georges Bresse, afire with the urge to serve, let it pass without comment, indeed without noticing. 'Lester Meyer wouldn't be easy to reach, men of his kind seldom walk alone. And in any case if we dealt with Meyer there'd be another to take his place at once. We know the race we're obliged to destroy.'

'So you think the key is his carriers?'

'Certainly. If a man close to Lester Meyer dies, violently and for no obvious reason, few others would be enthusiastic if Meyer approached them to smuggle out diamonds.' The *patron* waved an elegant hand, dismissing the matter as plainly established. They'd discussed it before, it was *res judicata*.

Nor did Bresse wish to discuss it again. Half a Marxist the dialectic had gripped him. The premises, the facts were established. It followed . . .

The *patron* was following on inexorably. 'And they can't use Pieter Brouwer again. He's marrying into the family, the husband of Lester Meyer's stepdaughter. It's inconceivable Lester Meyer would risk him.'

'That is true,' Bresse said and sincerely thought so. Another step in the ineluctable reasoning. 'Which brings us back to Maurice Pater.'

'I'm delighted that you follow me.' The *patron* spoke without hint of smugness, simply pleased that another could follow his mind. It didn't strike him as a house of cards where if one slipped the others collapsed untidily. The ratiocination was perfect.

More important, though he didn't know it, it meshed with his instincts and served his ends.

'There's one thing I'd like to be sure of,' Bresse said.

'By all means.' The *patron* tented his fingertips. He was the teacher meeting the student's sound point, the utterly devoted *chela*. The *patron* laid down what he knew was a trump. 'Just look at it from Meyer's viewpoint. Who could reasonably suspect Maurice Pater?'

Georges Bresse was impressed. 'That's a very strong point.' He was considering it when the *patron* went on.

'Of course if you want proof in a court, an enemy's court which we do not recognize. . . . But look at what we've just heard—that's final.'

'You mean that Pater's postponed his return? But he's going to visit a game reserve.'

'And why should a man like Pater do that? He isn't the kind to be keen on lions.' The *patron* shook his commanding head. 'It's irrelevant where he's chosen to go, what matters is that he's chosen to stay. His daughter has been safely married yet he's put off his return to England. Maurice Pater would never do that for a holiday, not in a country he's bound to detest.' The *patron*'s burning and faintly mesmeric stare focused sharply on Bresse's eyes and held them. 'If you don't want this mission then tell me straightly.'

'I didn't say that.'

The *patron* produced his final card, or what was final in his private reasoning. 'Then if Pater doesn't intend to help Meyer can you give me a single other reason which will cover the facts which this girl has reported?'

'Only guesses.'

'Who wants them?'

'Very good,' Bresse said, 'you may well be right.' He'd been thinking less frenetically but his conclusions had been much the same. The *patron* might perhaps be wrong, when Pater would die on a misunderstanding, but he was an enemy who had damaged the cause and who in England could damage the cause again. But if the *patron* was right and Georges Bresse refused he'd be a traitor to what he'd embraced and what drove him, no better than Said Abdul Jawal.

There was an instant and tangible relaxation. The *patron* smiled his electric smile, and Georges Bresse, decision made, unwound. He had known from the first it was inescapable.

He was sworn to this extraordinary man, he was his liegeman, his tool. That ended it.

The *patron* was saying: 'That leaves the details.'

'I've got a passport still. Not my own but a French one.'

'You'll need a visa—I'll fix that at once. Also a seat on the first flight possible.' He added with more than a hint of venom: 'Our enemies sneer that we're inefficient but in that sort of thing we're as good as they are, and in anything of real importance I know I can always rely on Georges Bresse.' The *patron* leant forward, the *coup d'œil* in top gear again. 'It isn't only that you know your job, you hold a French passport, you move quite freely. In South Africa that's a *sine qua non*, and I haven't another man I could send. The corollary you will grasp at once. There is only one chance in this matter—yours. Any failure will mean that Pater goes free, free to damage us as he pleases for ever.'

'I understand that.'

'I thought you would. Which brings up the matter of Pieter Brouwer.'

'But I thought you said——'

'I said that he wouldn't be used again in the matter of running diamonds out, I didn't say Meyer would never use him. He's an ex-policeman and wasn't selected for nothing. Maurice Pater, as a carrier, has advantages which Brouwer hasn't, but he also has disadvantages and Lester Meyer will be aware of them. In any sort of physical trouble Maurice Pater would be completely helpless. Lester Meyer knows this and I think he'll provide for it. Pieter Brouwer is the obvious choice.'

'But he's just got married.'

'I know he has. He's on honeymoon at Umhlanga Rocks, I learnt that from our usual source. That doesn't mean he's not available. An aircraft from Durban, a matter of hours...'

'You're suggesting I ought to deal with him first?'

'It's not for me to suggest a method. How you operate is

tactics, not strategy, and I'd never attempt to tie your hands. I can only say what I've said before. If you fail in this then I've nobody else and you know very well what we have at stake.'

'I take the point.'

'You'll think it over?'

'Yes,' Georges Bresse said, 'I'll think it over.'

15

In fact he had thought very hard indeed for he was far from the casual and heartless killer which Russell had suspected he might be and a pre-emptive murder was not his style. Said Abdul Jawal he considered no killing but simply a deserved execution, and he was fastidious in the use of violence, despising those who worshipped it and detesting men whom he knew were cruel. But the *patron* had nevertheless impressed him. If you accepted the *patron*'s logic at all then you had to accept the whole of it, and what he'd said at the end had been certainly true. Brouwer wouldn't be used as a runner again, but he'd been in the police, he was young and strong, and Georges Bresse had an excellent reason to know that Piet Brouwer was no fool with firearms. Next time he shot he might not be missing. It was true he was on his honeymoon, a long way from Pater's game reserve, but there were roads and fast cars and aeroplanes. Come to that Lester Meyer maintained his own. So Brouwer *could* be alerted, he *could* be recalled, and as Lester Meyer's private man he wouldn't be bound by the legal rules. Bresse couldn't be sure it would all go smoothly, he couldn't even be sure it had started smoothly. His enemies had a spider's web in almost every country on earth, and though his visa and the air-booking were in a name which was certainly not his own it wasn't inconceivable that this complex of often unpaid Intelligence had somehow contrived to pierce his cover. In which case they'd be waiting for him, but they wouldn't just have him arrested on landing, that wasn't the way they chose to work. To use a false passport earned several years' jail but they'd want more than that, they would want him disposed of. So they wouldn't just tip off the police, they'd wait; they'd wait till he put his head in their noose, then they'd tighten it and hang him finally. A dangerous ploy? Of course it was. Then if they knew at all that

L

Georges Bresse was coming they'd be covering every movement he made, not through the police but privately, and Piet Brouwer was the obvious man. So the *patron* had been right again. It would be over-insurance to kill Piet Brouwer apart from the fact it would also be murder, but it wouldn't be over-insurance to check, on the contrary it was a sane precaution. If Piet Brouwer had cut short his honeymoon then that would be significant. It would mean in fact that the trap was loaded, and in a country which he didn't know, where some slip could betray him and leave him helpless, there was only one way to be sure—to see. That meant visiting Durban first, a nuisance, but by the timetable of Pater's tour he had a day to do it and felt he must. To kill Pater he'd gladly lose life or liberty but he wouldn't just walk in a trap and fail.

Georges Bresse had never before been in Durban nor had time for what this mission demanded, a careful research and a detailed plan, but at the airport he'd bought a tourists' guide. On his entry form he'd put 'Royal Hotel' and as Reason for Visit 'Holiday'. He was thinking a little dourly now that one thing this trip wouldn't be was a holiday, for he didn't propose to stay at the Royal or indeed at any other hotel. But his guidebook had given him what he wanted, that the rich part of town was the Berea ridge, and from the airport he took a taxi there. He paid it off and began to walk, confident that in this opulent suburb a white stranger would attract no attention.

He found what he wanted in half an hour, a fine but unoccupied house with a garden. It was the sort of house which said money quite loudly, so the family would have gone to their beach-house or perhaps they had driven up to the Drakensberg. More important, there was a two-car garage, and one car, a Holden, was still inside it. Bresse had always intended to steal a car, but to take one from a street or park would have meant that the loss would be promptly reported, and with the number known he wouldn't get far. To be stopped by the police for stealing a hack would be both anti-climax and unprofessional, whereas by taking this Holden the chances were good. No doubt there would be an African caretaker but it was far from certain he'd check the garage, and Bresse didn't intend to smash his way in but to pick what he'd seen was a simple lock, then shut everything up as it had been before. So even if this African noticed he might not immediately think of theft; he might assume that one of the absent family had needed the second car and come back for it, and even if theft occurred to him he would hardly go to the police at once. Not an African to the local police. He'd telephone to his master first and he might not be able to contact him quickly. At the worst, Bresse decided, he had twenty-four hours and twenty-four hours was all he needed.

He hid in the garden and snatched some sleep, then when dusk came down he opened the garage. All this had been part of the plan he'd made and he'd brought what he needed for simple jobs with him. The car had no key but Bresse had many. He relocked the garage behind him and checked it, then he drove out to Pieter Brouwer's hotel. There was a risk that he'd be recognized but he thought it a very small one indeed. In any case he'd have to accept it, and he knew how to look and still stay inconspicuous. Just a glance on the terrace, in the bar, at the dining-room. If that yielded nothing he'd inquire at the desk, pretending to be a social journalist with a column for which he needed a piece. No doubt they would promptly send him packing but if they did so he'd know Pieter Brouwer was there still.

And it was on the way out to Umhlanga Rocks that the idea came from nowhere, a chance to escape. He had decided that he didn't have one, not after killing Maurice Pater. He was confident he could manage that but had accepted his capture as part of the price. Wherever he did it, day or night, in a sightseeing bus or in one of the rest camps, the place would be in an uproar at once, and even if he got away he had no place to hide in this frightening land. Every airport would be watched within minutes. But if he could make it look like an accident, not for ever of course but while they doubted and wondered. . . . If he could get to an airport before they blocked them . . .

He had considered all this and had seen no solution, but this new idea wasn't wholly impractical. It would be silent—guns weren't; it would give him time. Put to him by the *patron* in Paris he'd have dismissed it as an amateur's fantasy, but here in Africa, a revelation, it looked different, it was worth a try. If it failed he could always go back to the gun, he had nothing to lose and the chance of liberty. That is, if he could make himself do it. But this Georges Bresse sincerely doubted.

So he'd been driving out to Umhlanga Rocks when the idea had fallen out of the sky. On his right was a squat and whitewashed building, sinister at any time and in the unearthly light of the street lamps malignant. Georges Bresse read the notice, suppressed a shudder. He had a horror of what the building held.

Nevertheless, coming back from Umhlanga, he had made himself consider seriously. He would rather face torture again than that building, but he saw it as an obligation, the duty to survive if he could. And better what this building held than a life sentence in a foreign jail. In theory, that is, but this wasn't theory.

Georges Bresse was far from confident that he could drive himself to take what he must, but he went back to the house on the Berea ridge. It was a risk to return but he had to accept it: there were three things which he was going to need and in the garage there'd been a well-equipped work-bench. He picked the lock again and slipped in with a torch. He took a pair of welder's tongs from the bench and a fisherman's creel from a nail on the wall. From the garden he cut a long forked stick. Then he shut the garage door again and drove back to the North Beach, already shivering.

He parked the car and began a thorough reconnaissance. It was two in the morning and bleakly deserted, and there didn't seem to be any nightwatchman. (And who, Georges Bresse thought, would think one necessary?) The wall would be easy, he didn't fear it: what he feared was simply himself, Georges Bresse, his private and atavistic terror.

He sat down on the beach with a cigarette, disgusted that he could hardly light it. He'd been like this once before when they'd warned him. . . . Talk or in an hour we'll come back. And they had come back, he still bore the stigmata, but this was much worse since the choice was wider. . . . Talk—it had been unthinkable. But it wasn't unthinkable just to walk to the car, to drive to the Kruger and shoot Maurice Pater. It was in fact what he'd planned to do, but it would cost him his liberty, maybe his life, and it wasn't simply vanity to realize that the cause he loved had only a single Georges Bresse to serve it.

He rose at last and slipped over the wall. He knew exactly what he wanted to steal for his guidebook had had an excellent photograph. You couldn't mistake them, the white rings round the throat.

He shone his torch again and a shudder shook him. There was a sort of compound behind another low wall and in the beam of the torch he had seen what he wanted. The light woke it and it began to rear. He couldn't reach it with the tongs or the stick nor bring himself to step over the wall. Finally it began to move, away from the light of the torch, to a corner. Georges Bresse used the stick and then the tongs and when he'd done that the fisherman's creel. Georges Bresse would not have thanked you if you'd called him a very brave man indeed.

He climbed back across the outer wall, holding the creel away from him, running. He ran to the car and opened the boot throwing the creel inside, not looking. But he couldn't escape the noise it made, a scaly sort of angry slither.

Georges Bresse banged the boot and was brutally sick. He hadn't eaten since a meal on the aircraft and the vomit racked his stomach mercilessly. When he had finished he got back in the car.

He began to drive very fast indeed. Myself, he thought, and my friend behind me.

16

Charles Russell was in his modest hired car driving happily down to the Natal Midlands, a country whose rolling hills he loved and whose inhabitants he found congenial. He was driving as he always drove, fast but with a long experience, and was annoyed when the car behind him flashed. He was more annoyed when he heard the siren. He pulled in to wait and the police car passed him. It stopped in turn and a man got out quickly. He was a very large man and the figure familiar. The big man ran back to Russell's car.

'May I get in, please?'

'Certainly. Do.'

'Bad news,' the big man said.

'Then shoot it.'

'I'll tell it you as we pieced it together though that may not be the way it happened. You remember what I said about Pater, that we'd guard him till he flew out last night? Well, he didn't fly out, he cancelled his passage. Instead he's gone up to the Kruger Park. No reason given, no motive known. He didn't tell Mrs Meyer either. Now why do you think he did that?'

'I don't know.'

'Nor do I but it struck us as out of character—to dash off to the Kruger without telling anyone. I don't say I was worried yet, or I wasn't until I got a hunch.'

'We all of us get them. The wise ones listen.'

'So I followed this hunch and I really sweated. It started with something I just remembered, a remark of your own when we talked before. I was telling you someone had followed Pater and your question was: 'Rather a striking man? French accent?' It wasn't, it was only a girl, but it was clear you had such a one in mind. Now men with French accents aren't common here, and visitors who use French passports don't come in on every flight from Europe. So I

163

did a quick check on recent arrivals and a French passport came in at the airport yesterday.'

'The name was Georges Bresse?' Russell asked at once.

'Not on this passport but that means nothing. What's more ominous is that he flew on to Durban. He filled in the usual form on landing where he gave his address as the Royal Hotel. But he didn't check in there or anywhere else.'

Charles Russell thought it over quickly. 'There's no positive tie-up,' he said at length.

'I'm rather afraid there is—please hear me. Let's go back to that girl who followed Pater. I told you she was one of two sisters, Lebanese but there was nothing against them. But in the light of what's happened we followed that up, and the sister is a telephonist in the hotel where Maurice Pater was staying. And an hour after Pater had booked for the Kruger this sister is sending a full-rate cable. It reported where Maurice Pater was going and she sent it to an address in Paris.'

'Good enough,' Russell said, 'or rather bad.' A doubt struck him and he put it promptly. 'Durban's a very long way from the Kruger. But I suppose he could slip across the border, to Lourenço Marques, then rail to Machadodorp. Hire a car from there——'

But the big man was shaking his head emphatically. 'Too complicated and too much time. He hasn't flown on an aircraft—be sure he won't—but he could easily steal a car and drive.'

'You've checked on all stolen cars?'

'Of course. Since he landed we know of four in Durban, two Volkswagens and two British Minis. The numbers of all are also known and none of them will get near the Kruger.'

Charles Russell considered, he didn't like it, and not only for this good policeman's reasons. He knew something he didn't—it scared him severely; he knew the woman who now was Miriam Meyer.

'You said Pater went up to the Kruger Park without telling Mrs Meyer he'd done so.' Russell looked at the big man, watching his eyes; he didn't think he would lie and in fact he didn't. 'Have you told her since?'

'Yes I have. I had to.'

'I could wish that you hadn't.'

'I know what you mean, I do indeed. But for you it would be rather different. In England she'd just be Mrs Meyer but here she's Lester Meyer's wife.'

Russell said softly: 'You told her as cover if something went wrong?'

'You could call it that though it's not very friendly.'

'I understand,' Russell said. He thought again. 'May I ask what other steps you've taken?'

'I've sent two of my best men ahead by chopper.'

'Then I can't think of anything else.'

'I can.' The big man swung on his seat to face Russell. 'I'd like you to go to the Kruger too.'

Charles Russell was astonished and said so. 'Whatever for?'

'Just to be there yourself. In person.'

Now he wasn't astonished but sympathetic; he understood the big man perfectly. The big man wanted cover again. Maurice Pater was a Member of Parliament and if anything went badly wrong the ex-head of the Executive would be an independent but also friendly witness. Charles Russell smiled, he'd have done the same. 'Very well,' he said. 'If you think I could help.'

'I'm very grateful indeed.' The big man meant it. 'I suggest we take my car as the faster. My driver will bring yours back behind us.'

In the police car the big man said crisply: 'It's organized. Light aircraft first to a landing-strip. Car to meet us from there.'

'I'll need different clothes.'

'We'll call in at the Sunnyside.' The big man put his hand in his pocket. It came out with a pistol. He gave it to Russell.

'I'm not your third best man, you know. I'm a respectable retired official. I can see that I may have a use to you, but I've not fired a pistol for fifteen years.'

'No doubt you did once.'

'When I had to.'

'Just so. And I hope I needn't tell you that I'm coming on that aircraft too.'

'Three men and a boy and I'm the boy.' Russell looked at the pistol. 'Police issue?' he asked.

'I don't believe in handbag firearms.'

'But I think you're excessively optimistic. I couldn't hit a house today.'

'But at least you'll be armed.'

'I follow the thought.'

Russell followed the thought though he didn't much like it, but next day he was enjoying the Kruger since he wasn't obliged to force a choice between enjoyment and a nagging worry. That was the big man's business, not his. Words like virtue and defeat didn't come to him easily but it was sensible to seize the day. Moreover, he had no illusions; he hadn't been asked to come here for action but as insurance against this fine policeman's calamity. Charles Russell thought that sensible too. So why not enjoy the scene and the animals? Both were superb, both unmatched in Africa.

But it was habit still to observe one's peers and the big man's arrangements were reassuring. Dinner the night before had been covered, by a man at Maurice Pater's table who'd chatted pleasantly but been constantly wary, and when Pater had gone for a walk after eating another man rose from the *stoep* and went after him. Russell and the big man himself were sharing a *rondavel* together, and at intervals the light-sleeping Russell had been woken by soft-voiced consultations. The big man, it seemed, had a basic worry, that the perimeter fence was designed against animals but would be child's play for a determined man. And they couldn't patrol the whole of it, a circumference bigger than most English counties. What they could patrol was where Pater slept, where Pater ate and where Pater walked. Charles Russell had nodded. It was all very competent.

He confirmed it in the small bus next morning. There were fourteen persons and Russell could place them, five men and three women, all clearly tourists, and a sixth man who equally clearly wasn't. With Pater, the big man and Russell himself this dozen filled the pick-up's seats, and then there were the guide and the driver. The latter too had that smell of the police, unmistakable to the experienced nose. Russell had never met Maurice Pater but could identify him easily even without the guide's use of his name—obviously an Englishman, a hint of detachment, an air of worry. The guide was rather a good one and knowledgeable. Moreover, he didn't talk incessantly.

Russell gave himself up to quiet enjoyment. He'd shot animals as a younger man but now had lost the taste for it. No itch to kill disturbed his pleasure even if such a thing had been possible in an area where an African poaching could earn himself three to five years plus a beating. The only shooting here was the annual culling, for this wasn't a disappointing game park where the predators lived behind fences, fed daily. Here the predators preyed but not quite enough, and once or sometimes twice a year the commoner game was quietly thinned out. Charles Russell regretted the need to do so. The impala was his favourite beast with its aura of fastidious elegance and the poise of an almost arrogant sexiness. He'd seen much of this game in younger days but once, on a corner, they ran into elephant, two young bulls, showing off, which were slow to give way. And there were always the ubiquitous bush pig, supposedly symbols of everything ugly but Charles Russell found them entirely fascinating. Whole families ran in a file, father first, coiled sterns now erect, high-tailing it briskly. The monkeys you could have, he disliked them.

They lunched in one of the camps, quite well, and Russell noticed the drill with quiet approval. The driver stayed with the bus but the other man didn't, eating at Pater's table again, and on the veranda outside were two men with soft drinks, ostensibly from another party. After lunch they drove on in the mounting heat but when Russell nodded the big man woke him. He smiled a quick apology, but he needed Charles Russell awake and observant.

Back in the camp Russell went for a shower and the big man walked down to the pool for a bathe. When he returned he poured two drinks. No drink was on sale in these camps whatever but it was perfectly legal to bring it in. Russell hadn't known that but the big man had and he'd decently provided for both. He raised his glass.

'So far so good. Have you any hunch on it?'

'Out of my usual line, I'm afraid.'

'It's the old problem of the man with the gun. If he's determined enough to lose his own life it's the next thing to impossible to guarantee the life of his quarry.'

'From what I've observed you've done everything possible.'

'I'm glad you approve but there's always that loophole. We're in a corner here with a fence on three sides but if I were Bresse I wouldn't try here. There are a thousand places to hide a car, five miles away or even ten, so I'd hide my car and slip over somewhere. We'd need an army to cover the whole circumference. Then if an animal didn't get me walking here——'

'It's a pity that Pater is sleeping alone.'

'I know it is but I don't dare change it. He paid the extra for a single *rondavel* and he's the sort to kick if I slipped a man in. The *rondavel* is being watched of course, but it's not quite the same as a guard inside it.' The big man finished his whisky slowly. 'A dedicated man with a gun has always that outside chance or better.'

Charles Russell accepted this: it was true. 'Maurice Pater looks pretty peaked,' he said.

'He has the air of a worried man. . . . Your guess.'

'I haven't one, he can't know he's in danger.'

They had another drink, then Russell yawned. 'Enjoyable,' he said, 'but tiring.'

'Go to bed and I'll follow in half an hour. Just a last look round and a word with my people.' The big man hesitated, then said it firmly. 'Tomorrow the tourists go back to Johannesburg. It's got to be tonight or nothing.'

Russell brushed his teeth with his usual care. He had most of his own and was modestly proud of them, and the three which were not he put in permanganate. He went to his bed with a final whisky; he read for ten minutes and finished the drink; then he turned out the rather uncertain light. In four minutes he was fast asleep.

Three *rondavels* away Maurice Pater was not. Sleep wouldn't come and that was bad, but nor would ideas and that was worse. He had come to the Kruger for inspiration but not even a spark of that had been granted. . . . Twenty-one days he'd agreed with that lawyer, he had six of them left but the man had got restive. He'd even cabled, which Maurice Pater resented, since he'd have to tell Tuke the whole story or none, and if Tuke knew the pressure was on already. . . . There must be another plan . . .

There wasn't. He'd have to go to Tuke and hope, and Tuke was a man who might ask a price. Several were possible and all of them exigible.

He fell into restless sleep at last, but it was shallow and troubled and unrefreshing. In the distance there were alien noises, of the wild life about them perhaps, but not certainly, and at regular and maddening intervals there was a shuffle of careful feet past his hut. He had noticed a man whom he took for a sentry and the answer to his alarmed inquiry had been that thieves were his worry, not beasts breaking in. Mr Pater—a smile—could sleep in peace.

He could no doubt but in fact he wasn't. It was stifling in the thatched *rondavel* and he'd opened the top of the split loose-box door. He tossed and he muttered, half sleeping half conscious, and once he imagined he'd heard a noise, not the sounds of an animal world remote from him but something closer though he couldn't place it, a sort of slither, then a final soft bump.

He switched on the light but saw nothing at all, then he switched it off and somehow slept. A rat, of course, or something like it.

Ten minutes later he woke in fear. Something was on his bed. It had moved. That rat and he detested them. Through the half-open door came the moon's cool gleam, diffused but sufficient, more than sufficient. Maurice Pater sat up on the reflex of terror. This wasn't a rat.

Maurice Pater screamed.

Miriam Meyer was a determined woman but she respected her husband as well as loved him and she'd consulted him about the means. Neither had had the least doubt of the end and the aircraft was on its way already, but if Meyer rang Pieter it wouldn't look good, an inconsiderate order which might well be resented. After all Piet was on his honeymoon. Whereas if Miriam Meyer rang her daughter and the daughter in turn told a loving husband that husband could hardly decline to help when it was father-in-law who was clearly in danger.

So when the telephone rang Pieter said: 'It's your mother. She wants you and something's happened—bad.' He passed the receiver, watched Barbara's face, first astonished, then frightened, then finally grim. Still holding the line she explained to him shortly.

'Where did this story come from?' he asked.

'The police found out.'

'Then the police will be watching it.'

'Of course they will but it's not enough.'

'Who thinks so?'

'My mother.'

He thought it over, rubbing his chin. Pieter wasn't afraid of Miriam Meyer but had an excellent motive to keep her respect. 'When's this aircraft arriving?'

'It's flying already.' She spoke into the phone again. 'Landing in Durban in less than an hour.'

'Very well, I'll be on it. And damn their eyes.'

He started to pack as she told her mother. He didn't take much but he took his gun.

17

Russell reached the door first but only just, the big man a couple of strides behind him. Pater's screams were almost continuous now, a crescendo of naked animal fear. The camp had begun to wake and stir and in the compound a man was running fast. He saw Russell and shouted in Afrikaans, then he shouted again in English: 'Halt!' Charles Russell went on at a steady lope and a bullet came past his ear with a whine. He heard the big man's furious roar behind him, in Afrikaans too and it wasn't courteous.

He slipped the bolt of the lower half of the door and the beam of his torch caught the bed and held it. Pater was silent now, exhausted, frozen in terror's final extremity. The snake had already reared, was weaving. The big man at Russell's shoulder said: '*Rinkhals.*'

It meant nothing to Russell, the snake's hood did. He said to the big man: 'Take the torch, keep the beam on it,' then he brought up the pistol and called on his God. He had a line of fire without killing Pater, but he hadn't fired pistols for fifteen years and the snake had begun to weave again. It was swaying its head perhaps six inches, the white bands on its throat were livid weals. Russell aimed for the forward swing and fired. The snake's head disappeared but a second too late. Pater had put his hands to his eyes. He wasn't screaming now but had started to whimper. 'It's blinded me,' he said. 'Oh God.'

The big man took over fast and smoothly. '*Rinkhals,*' he said again, 'the spitter. Strikes too but it hadn't time for that. Marvellous shot, by the way.'

'A fluke.'

'So now we'll have to wash his eyes out. I saw you had permanganate—use it. I'll send in a man who knows the drill.'

The big man went out at a powerful double and another came in and nodded briefly. 'I heard talk of permanganate.'

'Yes, in my hut.'

Together they washed out Pater's eyes. He was moaning, utterly passive, helpless. The newcomer was cool and expert. Charles Russell asked him: 'Are you a doctor?'

'No, they train us in first aid a bit.'

'If you'd care to explain—I'm quite at sea.'

'The snake you mean? Where's what's left of it?'

'I think it fell under the bed.'

'I'll get it.'

'I'd really prefer that you didn't do that.'

'Then white bands round the throat?'

'That's right. And a hood.'

'The spitting cobra—extremely dangerous. Not a true *naja*, I'm told, but worse. Bite poisonous, spit highly toxic. It could permanently damage the sight if you don't do something about it quickly. Incidentally it's not a native up here. Somebody must have slipped it in.' The policeman looked at Pater reflectively. 'His eyes will be all right, I'm sure, but he's shocked and pretty close to collapse. There's a hospital twenty miles from here and we'll move him there by car at once.'

Outside there were two shots, then a third.

Georges Bresse had been driving against the clock, stopping only when hunger forced him to, at a roadhouse for beer and a plate of sandwiches. It was essential that he reach the Kruger before a second night came and made recce impossible, for though night would be his powerful ally it would be an enemy if he arrived in the dark, still in ignorance of the actual layout. In fact he gave himself rather more than this and was happy to accept the gift, for he was working under a disadvantage which he hadn't had time or the means to remove. That disadvantage was the lack of a map, or rather of a proper one. There'd been an office in Paris which had probably had one, but the *patron* had been suspicious and stubborn, forbidding what he considered the risk of an inquiry for a foreign map, and in Durban Georges Bresse hadn't dared to go shopping. What he had was what he'd picked up at the airport, a tourist brochure about the Kruger Park, adequate to its ends, full of colour, but the map, if you could call it that, was little better than a diagram. It showed the boundaries of the Reserve itself, the locations of the various rest camps, and the roads between them as dotted lines. Very dotted, Bresse thought, and quite unreliable. The most this plan showed was that roads existed, and Georges Bresse must do what he could with that. With that and his own essential reconnaissance.

His first objective was the principal rest camp since it was very long odds most tours would be based there, which meant it was where Maurice Pater would sleep. The diagram showed it quite close to the fence, and as Bresse hid in the scrub and used his glasses, changing his position often, he could piece together the general layout without going inside or even trying to. He had never had any intention of trying. These camps were booked solid for months ahead and very few visitors came on chance, so any questions would look naïve at best and from a man with a foreign accent peculiar. He might even arouse some warden's suspicion and that was the last thing he wished to risk.

Bresse walked back to where he'd left his car, a good mile from the gate and off the road. . . . So far so good but it wasn't much. His plan was in fact as the big man had guessed it, to skirt round the fence for several miles, then slip over and follow a road to the rest camp. It sounded simple in theory: Georges Bresse knew it wasn't. This was bush and he hadn't been trained to use it, and he knew that he wouldn't be walking alone. He had a weapon but so had the other prowlers; he had a pistol but those others had silence. He could be jumped from the back and know nothing about it, and his end would be neither quick nor clean.

He suppressed the thought since he had others more practical. He had left his car at a junction of tracks, where they joined with the road to the gate, branching from it. He had a mapping-board, paper fixed already, a good compass and his car's milometer. He took a bearing and carefully marked the camp, then he tossed for the tracks, right or left. Left won.

Georges Bresse began to plot his movement since if he didn't he knew that he'd lose himself hopelessly. Sometimes he could see the fence but more often the bush or a low hill hid it. Four furlongs on the speedometer. Stop. Take a bearing and enter the plot. Go on. The track was swinging northwards now and the diagram showed the fence did too. Georges Bresse had been scared he'd make too much westing and he hadn't had sight of the fence for some time, but he drove on now, plotting still but more confident, and presently he saw it again, on his right, in the fading light, but there. He looked at his plot and he looked at the dashboard. Seven miles in a very wide right-hand bend, say four and a half from the camp directly. Not that directness was much in point—to walk blind in this bush by night would be madness—but if his plot was right and he thought it was there'd be a road here a mile inside the wire and that road would lead back to the camp and Pater.

There were some trees whose names he didn't know and in them he hid the car. He slept.

He had always been able to wake as he wished and three hours later he did so, refreshed. He climbed the fence with his creel and walked steadily east, at first reassured for this wasn't too bad. The moon was brighter than he'd expected it, the country more open—it gave him a chance. He might be charged by a lion but he wouldn't be jumped, he had a chance to reach the road in safety. That wouldn't be final—no, very far from it—but at least it would be something familiar.

175

He had gone what he guessed was half-way to the road when he realized just how treacherous his diagram for tourists was. Tourists drove in motor cars, not interested in much else but the game. So this diagram had had pictures of elephants but it hadn't shown much of what mattered to Bresse.

Particularly not this appalling water. It was less than a river but more than a stream and clearly it wasn't some sort of pond. It moved. Very sluggishly, with its own dark menace. It would be futile to try to work round it. Over? There wasn't a hint of a crossing. Then through. . . .

Georges Bresse had stopped dead, his stomach freezing. A lion he would have faced if he must, but what lived in an African water . . . God. The sudden snap and the swirl of a dark-stained water, the agonizing and merciless death. A few hours ago he'd drawn deep on his courage: there was little left, he must overdraw. He made himself tie the creel to his waist. He was a Muslim now but had quite forgotten. Instinctively he crossed his breast, then he lowered himself in the water and swam. Once he touched a log and choked hard on a scream. It was only ten strokes but it seemed like an ocean. When he was over he almost collapsed.

He sat down to rest but soon looked at his watch, and after ten minutes he rose, still shivering. He walked for twenty minutes more, then the road came up at him unexpectedly. He began to relax and turned south; he went on.

. . . The first hurdle behind me but only the first.

If Georges Bresse had had charge of this comfortable rest camp he wouldn't be leaving a road wide open which led straight into sleeping tourists' quarters, so if this one were blocked or perhaps patrolled it wouldn't be an unwelcome omen that the camp was alerted against his coming. In any case he was little concerned since he didn't propose to use the road once he sensed that he was near to the camp; and he had more than his senses to warn him of that—the cigarette carton thrown in the dust by the roadside, the signs that the bush had been thinned and tamed, the indefinable but growing instinct that he was closing on where men lived and slept. He stepped off the road and went back to the bush.

He'd no experience of the African bush but had been taught to move quietly at night and did so. It wasn't difficult here for the moon was still strong and in perhaps fifty yards he saw the fence, not the main one round the Reserve's perimeter but enough to discourage a curious animal. He examined it for an alarm-wire but saw none, and in any case he must take the risk. He climbed it and walked on steadily till he came to the first of the camp's *rondavels*. Presumably these were the servants' quarters and Bresse threaded between them with mounting care. Africans, he knew, woke early. He was now on the opposite side of the camp from where he had made his inspection through glasses, but this had told him that there was a central compound with the better *rondavels* grouped around it. The brick building before him must be the showers. He slipped into it for a final reconnaissance.

Bresse had still to solve his most serious problem, that he didn't know where Maurice Pater was sleeping, but his hope had been there'd be something to show him, a bigger *rondavel* for V.I.P.s, one with a private bathroom to mark it.

They all looked the same to Georges Bresse. He frowned.

Then he saw it and relaxed again. One of the huts was patrolled by a sentry, not one of the African guards whom he'd noticed, men with shotguns or nightsticks and boots against snakes, but a white man who wore a wide belt and a holster. He was pacing a regular sentry's beat and it seemed he had very careful orders. As he passed the *rondavel* he lifted his feet. He mustn't disturb the V.I.P.

Georges Bresse who'd been holding his breath let it out. He was excited and eager and picked up the creel, and promptly he made his first mistake. He walked out of the showers and straight into an African. He hadn't heard him or even sensed he was near. The man wore boots but with rubber soles and he'd been moving like the black shadow he threw. As for the sense of a human presence Georges Bresse's excitement had put it to sleep.

If the African guard had seen Bresse first, raising an instant alarm by shouting, his mission would have aborted at once, but the fact that a stranger walked straight in his arms left him silent for a vital second. An astonished mouth opened to yell: Bresse shut it. He took the voice from the yell with a fist in the stomach and as the African's head jerked forward chopped him. He went as limp as a string and Georges Bresse caught his fall. He pulled him silently into the showers, put him down.

. . . Not so good, you were lucky. Next time be more careful.

He began to watch the sentry hard, timing his beat against his watch. The man was striding it deliberately, almost ceremonially—forty paces exactly in thirty-four seconds. It wasn't a lot, it would have to do. Bresse waited till one beat was ended, the end nearer the showers where Bresse was hiding. The man turned his back and Bresse picked up his creel. He was shoeless now and the soft dust helped him. When the guard passed the thatched *rondavel*'s door Georges Bresse was as close as he dared, ten paces. The guard had twenty to go which was seventeen seconds.

The door was half open, the luck was still with him. . . . Open the creel and tip the snake out of it. Slide round to the back of the hut and wait. . . .

The policeman turned and came back without even a glance. He was doing what he'd been told to do and in his days in the army he'd done it often. When he'd reached the far end of his beat again Georges Bresse could go back to the showers and safety.

Comparative safety, he thought with a smile, for he

didn't intend to walk back through the bush. There was an hour or two to daylight still, he could chance the main fence and the track directly. Seven miles to his car on a route he'd plotted, then if the gods were kind a dash to Johannesburg. If the gods were even kinder still there'd be a chance that they wouldn't have blocked the airport.

He walked silently out of the showers with the creel since to leave it might start a train of thought which he didn't wish any policeman to follow and slipped down past the pool to the outer fence. If his plot had been anything like correct then the track would at this point run very close.

Georges Bresse began to climb the fence, but at the top of it, one leg over, he froze. He'd seen something he hadn't expected to see. There was a car by the track and a man fast asleep in it.

Piet Brouwer left Durban some time after Bresse but his journey had been a great deal quicker, to the same airstrip Charles Russell had used with the big man, then a car again and a driver waiting. Piet Brouwer had dismissed him at once. If anything really came out of this two men would be an embarrassment.

He was inclined to think that nothing would. There'd been some excellent police work, some sane precautions, but it was hard to see what one man could do, even a dangerous man like Bresse. Piet believed they were over-playing it, and to call him back from a honeymoon was something which he thought close to panic. But he started the car and he drove to the Kruger.

Where they wouldn't even let him in. The gate was controlled by a regular policeman, not the warden he'd always seen before, and though it was one whom Pieter knew he wouldn't move an inch or compromise. Not even on Lester Meyer's name. He had his orders—they weren't elastic: no admissions till further notice—none. Then would he ring to his superior? No. The man who was running this operation was much too senior to chance a liberty, but in the morning, if nothing had happened, he'd tell him; he'd report Piet's arrival and ask for instructions.

Piet saw that he wouldn't change his mind, so he did what Georges Bresse had done before him, took the track to the left for a mile but halted. There was nothing to do so Piet Brouwer slept.

And half across the fence Bresse saw him—the car, and though the moon was fading, a man who was fast asleep in it. This was a piece of luck, indeed. It was seven good miles to Georges Bresse's Holden and seven good miles were perhaps two hours. And hours could be important now.

He wouldn't need to kill this man to take his car and increase his chances.

He had both feet on the ground when the camp exploded. Behind him he heard a shot, then shouting, a confusion of running feet, an uproar.

Bresse hadn't expected that so soon. When he'd tipped the snake into Pater's hut it had seemed sluggish, even comatose, and Bresse had not been inclined to blame it. He knew nothing about its habits whatever, but it hadn't been fed for twenty-four hours and he'd dragged it through an African river. He had thought it would probably rest for a bit, but clearly it hadn't. Very clearly.

That was awkward but it wasn't fatal, especially with this gift from heaven, another car which he hadn't dreamt he'd find. The noise from the camp had woken the man in it and he was climbing out, a little stiff. He hadn't yet seen Georges Bresse.

He suddenly did.

. . . . It all depends what this man does next. If he simply starts talking, says: 'What's going on?'. . . .

Brouwer looked at Georges Bresse and Georges Bresse looked back. Neither could see the other's face but Piet

Brouwer could guess and Georges Bresse could not. Brouwer stiffened; he put a hand in his pocket.

. . . . The man is a policeman, a picket. *He knows.*

For the first and last time Georges Bresse lost his head and no man of his trade would be found to condemn him. With success just behind him, escape so near. . . .

He pulled his pistol and he started shooting. The first smashed the windscreen of Pieter's car, the second found Pieter Brouwer's left shoulder. It spun him but it was also too late. Piet had already fired. Just once.

Once was enough. Georges Bresse stopped shooting.

The big man was back at the door of the hut. He was stained with sweat but he wasn't panting. 'Someone's been shot climbing out from the wire. I've looked at him—he's a European.'

'Dead?'

'Very nearly. He's talking French.'

'I'll come,' Russell said.

'I'd be very grateful.'

They ran down past the bath to a knot of men. Pieter Brouwer was standing aside, arm dangling. There were the last of the moon and lamps and torches, and in a pool of light a man was lying. Under him was a blanket, reddening. Russell knelt down beside him quietly. 'Georges Bresse,' he said. 'We meet again.'

The glazing eyes opened and finally focused. *'Mon colonel,'* Bresse said. He was almost gone.

'Is there anything I can do?'

'Perhaps.'

'Then tell me.'

Bresse told him.

'I'll do my best.'

Bresse held out his hand and Russell took it. He held it until Georges Bresse was dead.

18

It was the same Italian restaurant where Pater had dined before he'd been followed but Charles Russell was now entertaining Miriam. He had rung her from the Kruger Park and Miriam had been out to the hospital where Pater was recovering slowly. Slowly and it seemed reluctantly. His eyes were nearly normal again, there wouldn't be any permanent damage, but he'd been savagely shaken and he wasn't resilient. It was a pleasant little hospital in the heart of well-watered orange country and Miriam had visited more than once. The third time the doctor had led her aside. 'I'm not happy,' he said, 'he's not really responding.'

'It was a serious shock for any man.'

'Indeed it was but he's perfectly sound, in fact for his age he's remarkably healthy.' The doctor looked down but he finally said it. 'It's almost as though he wasn't trying.'

'Trying to get well, you mean?'

'No, trying to face the world again.'

Miriam hadn't answered him but she was talking to Charles Russell freely. But first she had wanted his view and had asked for it.

'Will Maurice be perfectly safe here now?'

' "Perfectly" is a very big word but clearly he's safer here than most places.' Charles Russell considered carefully for one didn't talk loosely to Miriam Meyer. 'To start with Georges Bresse was quite exceptional, an exceptional man if you look at it one way, and certainly an exceptional agent. I doubt if they've got another like him and if they haven't Georges Bresse was their only hope here. In England it would be rather different since their race can come in and out at pleasure. And there's your own police to consider on top of that. They haven't approved of what's happened at all so if Maurice does stay be sure of one thing. Nothing like that will be likely again.'

'That's excellent,' she said, 'since he's staying.'

'You persuaded him?'

'No, Charles—compelled him. That's why he's sulking in bed, not trying. He simply won't face the idea of it. The doctor doesn't know that since of course I've not told him.'

'The man's an adult,' Russell said severely, 'an adult male of legal age.'

'And when you've said that what *have* you said?'

'What you told me once—you haven't changed much.'

'I'm not defending what I've done. I don't need to.'

'Mother knows best?'

'Of course she does.' There'd been a note of faint asperity but she relaxed at once with her friendly smile. 'Would you care to hear?'

'If you'd care to tell me.'

She told him about the solicitor, the twenty-one days, her own manœuvres.

'So when he got that telegram he went up to the Kruger to think it over?'

'And how should I know he'd do that?' she asked.

'Suppose he'd come back in one piece as intended?'

'Then I'd have thought up some fiddle to keep him here till the twenty-one days were safely over and the money was firmly here in his bank. Lester and I didn't find that difficult. I'd been intending to use what had really happened, the whole story which Maurice still doesn't know, as an argument to persuade our Maurice, but he's sick in bed, I couldn't do that, so we used it on the lawyer instead. We told him something of the actual politics. Not everything—we didn't need to. He went up like a torch for he's very respectable. He couldn't get rid of the money fast enough, and once it was here in Maurice's name Maurice couldn't go back, not Maurice Pater.'

'You were sure of that?'

'Of course I was. You know Maurice Pater and I know him better.'

'At any rate it worked,' Russell said.

'Then why are you looking worried.'

'Am I? I'd rather you called it reflective.'

'Tell me.'

Instead he asked another question. 'So that money is really here?'

'Indeed. In a bank in his name, all open and legal. And Lester has found him a pretty good job. In England he was finished anyway. I've got politics in my blood, you see, and he couldn't have ridden the wind for a month. They'd have dropped him in the dustbin on the first excuse Harry Tuke could have found. His majority was a cool ten thousand and that's more than a suspect backbencher should have.'

Charles Russell said with a hint of irony: 'And later, when he's settled down, you'll be considering finding a suitable wife?'

The irony Miriam Meyer ignored. 'I think it's a little early for that.'

'But no doubt you've got someone in mind.'

'I've got two.'

'Christ almighty in heaven.'

'You forget I'm a Jewess.'

'That's one thing I don't.' Unconsciously Russell echoed her husband. 'I wouldn't fancy you as an enemy.'

'Thank you.'

He paid the bill and they walked to Miriam's car. 'I'll drive you back to the Sunnyside Park.'

'That's really very kind. I'm forgiven?'

'Would you care if you weren't?'

'Very much indeed.'

He watched her drive fast but always admirably. When the traffic had thinned she turned and asked him:

'A penny for what you're thinking.'

'Twopence.'

'Blackmail again but I'll have to pay.'

'Are you happy with Lester?'

'I'm very happy. Why do you ask it now, Charles Russell?'

'I was thinking about a town called Venice.'

'I'm getting a little old for that.'

'I don't think you're getting old for anything.'

'You're really very charming.'

'No.'

'You weren't making a pass?'

'Indeed I was. The motive might surprise you, though.'

'And now,' she said, 'comes the slap in the face.'

'And now,' he said, 'comes the biggest compliment. The motive was curiosity—partly. I was wondering what bed would be like with a woman of whom you were horribly frightened.'

Harry Tuke was accustomed to hide his depression but he'd listened to Russell and now wasn't trying. 'It's a perfectly bloody world,' he said.

'Have you only discovered that today?' Russell for once was distinctly short. He had landed that morning and slept poorly on aircraft.

'I'll stand anything but philosophy, Charles.'

'Frankly, I think you've been rather lucky. You were worried that Pater would split your Party, then when war came and a split was inevitable you started worrying he'd create a scandal. That won't happen now, I've just told you why, but you never considered Maurice Pater. And now he's safely in South Africa——'

'Is he?'

'You're slipping, Harry—what question is that? Is he in South Africa? Certainly. Or is he safe there? Yes, I think so.'

'Stop tutoring me, I'm not in the mood.'

'And I need a drink. I'll buy you one.'

They went to Charles Russell's club and the whisky, two establishment and established figures, both elderly but both far from senile. Tuke mellowed first. 'I'm sorry I snapped.'

'I wasn't exactly sympathetic but I still think you're very fortunate. You've heard the last of a man who was causing you worry and would probably have caused you more. Now he'll give up his seat and that's what you wanted.'

'But I still think it's an appalling world. I wasn't considering Maurice Pater, I was thinking about the Middle East. I doubt if what's happened means major war, just indefinite guerrilla beastliness.'

Charles Russell didn't answer this since 'beastliness' was unconscious patronage. If you'd lost your land, your home, your roots, if you'd been born in some squalid camp and raised there, kept alive by the conscience of other nations, then revenge was your only hope and stay. Beastly? Revenge was certainly always that but blind condemnation was worse—it was stupid. It could leave you with blunted weapons too, since even a laughably feckless people were human still and could learn from experience. The organization Georges Bresse had worked for was weak and divided, a rather poor joke. It wouldn't remain a joke for ever. As experience grew so would boldness also, these men would increase and flourish mightily. The States which claimed them would always stay divided since no power short of conquest would ever unite them, but the men themselves would find self-respect and they'd never felt bound by alien laws. So there'd be piracies and kidnappings and an astonished world wouldn't know the answer. Shocking breaches of international law? Of course they would be and what of that? Arab eternally fighting Arab, States which encouraged then pulled out the props. Naturally you'd rely on yourself, think of new techniques and apply them ruthlessly. The conventional would wring helpless hands, resentful of what was outside the rules, but if your homes had been wretched, the land ill cared for, what answer was that to the men who had lost them, what answer that another race had watered your desert and made it bloom? So States would decay and two thrones might fall but the men who would follow Georges Bresse might succeed.

Charles Russell sighed for he wasn't a prophet, only a man who had seen much life. Harry Tuke had condemned it as very ill-organized and at sixty Charles Russell would not dissent. It was better instead not to think of abstractions but of the people who'd somehow snatched at contentment, the lucky ones who had reached the lifebelts. Lester Meyer who'd broken some rules he despised, but that risk was over, he'd done what he must. Pieter Brouwer who'd done his simple duty and Barbara who'd made a brave new life in a country which would soon accept her. But Georges Bresse was the happiest man of all. Georges Bresse was at peace. Georges Bresse was dead.

He had died with his head in Russell's arms, talking French in an expiring whisper, asking an enemy's final favour. He'd been a Muslim now for several years but when it came to the crunch he couldn't face it. In a Muslim country perhaps— yes, certainly—but not in this bitterly foreign soil. The only link here was the church he'd been born in. So send for a priest and bury me decently.

Russell had promised he would and had done so.

He smiled as he remembered it for the priest had been an African but wise in the ancient unchanging disciplines. . . . This man had been baptized a Catholic? Russell had said he'd been born a Frenchman and his mother had been a Christian too. And as he'd died he had asked for Christian burial? Yes, that was so, Charles Russell had heard it. The African had nodded politely. *Nihil obstat?* he'd thought, but he'd said: 'I'll arrange it.'

Russell ordered more whisky as he thought of the others.

Miriam Meyer whom no disaster dared wound, the big man with his strong deep roots. Maurice Pater . . .

Maurice Pater would settle down in time—in time he might even achieve some happiness. Not a lot, Maurice Pater would hardly attract it. But in a real sense he was a lucky man.